Alex Carter has worked in, around, and for large corporations and government bureaucracies for decades, humorously capturing the essence of 'cubicle life' in his first novel, *Chip Clementine and the October Surprise*. When not thinking about Chip's latest adventures and mishaps, Alex loves cooking, being around family, serving in the U.S. Army Reserve as a 'corporate strategist,' and generally finding ways to fight off the aging process. He lives in North Carolina with his wife and extended family.

To the love of my life, my wife, Annette.

Alex Carter

CHIP CLEMENTINE AND THE OCTOBER SURPRISE

AUSTIN MACAULEY PUBLISHERS™

LONDON * CAMBRIDGE * NEW YORK * SHARJAH

Ordering Information
Quantity sales: Special discounts are available on quantity purchases by corporations, associations, and others. For details, contact the publisher at the address below.

Publisher's Cataloging-in-Publication data
Carter, Alex
Chip Clementine and the October Surprise

ISBN 9781647501891 (Paperback)
ISBN 9781647501884 (Hardback)
ISBN 9781647501907 (ePub e-book)

Library of Congress Control Number: 2021909699

www.austinmacauley.com/us

First Published 2021
Austin Macauley Publishers LLC
40 Wall Street, 33rd Floor, Suite 3302
New York, NY 10005
USA

mail-usa@austinmacauley.com
+1 (646) 512-5767

This book has been a work in progress for a long time, stuck in my mind until the last few years when I received some timely advice that helped me visualize how I should frame this story and start writing. For this reason, my daughter, Hali, gets her own paragraph.

After having read some of my early attempts at bringing *Chip Clementine* to life, she said to me that what I had was just a collection of anecdotes and not a book and that I needed a plot to make it…well, a book.

She was right and I thank her for nudging me into shaping *Chip Clementine* into a novel of sorts.

Writing this book took longer than I thought but more rewarding than I could have ever imagined. My mum has been my constant supporter throughout this process. Her critical eye and numerous edits motivated me to finish the initial manuscript.

My son-in-law, Regan, is also a big fan of this book and also helped me considerably.

My dad and my sister were both diagnosed with cancer, pancreatic and breast, respectively, while I was writing this book. Both are alive today – thanks to surgery, iron will, some luck, and many prayers. Their struggles and challenges throughout their surgery and recovery inspired me, more than any other factor, to bring this book to life and be a source of joy and humor for those that may be going through some of their darkest times.

Last but not least, I thank my beautiful, loving wife, Annette, for supporting me through this journey. She is my rock and without her, I would not have attempted, much less written this book.

I have spent a lifetime compiling these vignettes and shaping them into a story and a message that I hope will inspire as well as entertain. I hope Chip will give you the lift when you need it the most. He did for me.

About this Book

When middle-aged office accountant Chip Clementine is told he has breast cancer, his controlled life goes off-orbit as he gets to grips with his new normal.

Ever the opportunist, Chip processes his shock and channels his grief the only way he knows how – taking advice from those he trusts, finding new friends in the most unusual of places, having a bit more fun at the office, pulling overnighters at work, brokering deals for those less confident, and, of course, signing up for a flash mob dance at his local mall.

It isn't until after his first cancer-support group meeting that he realizes what's truly important and how his 'October Surprise' can reset his outlook on life.

Laugh, cry, and cheer with Chip as he navigates the spectrum of human drama at work with his cubicle colleagues on the fourth-floor.

Learn about his past before he entered the corporate scene. Be inspired by his unconventional fitness program. Take heart when he confronts the I.T. guy with no social filters. Empathize when Chip's eye twitch takes on a life of its own. Silently cheer with him when he finds the courage to reach out to another in a moment of panic when a routine MRI scan goes pear-shaped.

Experience Chip's day at the office with insights and observations that will make you giggle and fall off your ergonomically designed chair. Share in his quiet victories and feel a kinship with him when he takes one for the team. Even a cancer diagnosis doesn't stop Chip from giving you a comedic lift and an emotional nudge.

My goal is simple – to make you smile, chuckle, or laugh if only for a few moments a day during a particularly rough week. You always have Chip.

Alex Carter
Apex, North Carolina
2021

"We were together.
I forget the rest."

– Walt Whitman

Excerpt from Chip Clementine and the October Surprise

The boss stood up from his chair, took a deep breath and looked around. This was his first big meeting as a newly-hired manager and only just recently graduated from business school with an MBA and an attitude. Barely one month into his new job, his time had come to shine, and he was not going to fail. He had prepared, rehearsed, and even dressed for this event. It was times like this when others would look to their leader (him) to take them through this crisis.

"Okay, settle down. Well, things aren't looking too good, folks. The front office is telling us we're not making our numbers."

He had read somewhere that saying 'folks' made him more approachable. Of course, that only worked on a few of the 'folks' in the room, mainly the older crowd that was near retirement and couldn't care less what any manager would say in any meeting.

Meetings for them were reasons to catch up with other 'folks' they hadn't seen in a while. It was a big company so when meetings like this happened it was a thing.

Most saw the boss for what he was – another aloof, distant, calculating, opportunistic manager fresh from B-school out to make a mark in his first rung on the corporate ladder.

He paused for effect, but it didn't do any good. He could see it in their eyes. He kept going like he was reading from a script which he was because he had the notecards, typed notecards with lots of underlines and exclamation points – prompts for someone that needed to be prompted.

Chip had never seen a manager with typed notes on notecards and Chip had seen his share of new managers come and go over the years. *Impressive*, Chip thought. The boss cleared his throat.

"So...I know we're accountants and don't do any of the selling, but we can always cut expenses and help out with trimming the bottom line. So, I need each of you to put your good idea hats on and shout out some ways we can save money for the company. Who wants to start?"

The boss had his assistant near him with a magic marker and a whiteboard. She was there to capture all of the good ideas and make sure the boss got credit for all of them.

Chip's nameless boss scanned the crowd. There was a long, long pause – *too long*, the boss thought. Chip wasn't surprised. This late in the afternoon, with post-lunch fatigue setting in, there would be no good idea hats to be found in this group. Ideas were always in short supply with accountants after lunch.

Then a voice penetrated the auditorium. "Cut the air conditioning!" Chip said it out loud without thinking. Sometimes, he couldn't tell if he had used his outside voice or inside voice. This should have been his inside voice. It wasn't, it so wasn't.

"Who said that?" the boss said. The rest of the auditorium reacted with a steadily increasing volume of boos, hisses, and wailings. The crowd's reaction took Chip back a little, but he was ready for them.

Chip always thought the company could save money through better climate-control practices and he was ready for anyone to challenge him on it. Chip always had ideas, unusual for a middle-aged accountant with no prospects for advancement.

"Me, Chip Clementine – Accounting, fourth-floor."

He said it slowly because when he said 'accounting' slowly, everyone who wasn't an accountant automatically thought what had been said by that person was beyond reproach and of the highest fidelity. They were accountants after all – the stewards of the company's innermost secrets and guardians of the corporate keep.

He didn't have to say which department or what floor; everyone knew Chip was an accountant and they were on the fourth-floor. Some wished they weren't. Not Chip. He was a die-hard fourth floorer.

"Surely the air conditioning won't get cut," they whispered. Heads turned left, right, up, and down. Some heads turned all the way around and then back again.

A woman in the back of the auditorium fainted but no one bothered to help. Sally had a history of fake fainting. She'd fake fainted before and most thought this was another attention-getting move for all the wrong reasons.

So, ignoring Sally, they waited for what the boss would say next.

"Chip, I need serious ideas. Anyone else?" The boss was hoping for participation but not the kind that came from Chip. That was just nuts. Cutting the air-conditioning was not the kind of suggestion he could work with.

Without permission, his assistant wrote the words 'CUT A/C' in big, bold, blue letters on the whiteboard. The assistant had great penmanship and didn't make the rookie move of using the wrong colors to write with. Even the folks in the very back of the auditorium could see it.

The boss turned around and saw what she'd done but couldn't tell her to erase it. It was too late for that. The genie was out of the bottle. The notecards had outlived their usefulness. He was on his own now.

"Come on, people! I'm not kidding. Do you think I enjoy these meetings?" Chip heard giggles off to the right, and so did Peter, the boss who was now named.

It was clear who was really in charge and it wasn't the guy standing next to a portable whiteboard with an assistant. Chip piped up again, "Peter, if you are serious about saving, then cutting the air conditioning is the only way to make an impact."

Chip knew the game he was playing. Peter didn't like to be called Peter either. Peter was his first name but preferred his middle name.

Most people didn't address him by his first or middle name. They preferred no name, just his title – it made things easier for them when lines were drawn between management and the workers.

"Okay, I get it," Peter said, trying to sound confident. Peter didn't get it. Peter continued, "That's a little extreme, but thanks for your input, Chip. Any other ideas?"

Total silence. Peter's palms were getting sticky and he wondered if anyone could see his right eye twitch.

Meanwhile, most thought that with Peter's dismissal of Chip's idea, such an extreme measure was off the table. *Crisis averted!* they thought. Keeping the air conditioning meant they would enjoy a constant 68 degrees while surfing the net in their tiny cubicles. Life would go on uninterrupted.

Surely, they thought, *someone else would offer up another more-acceptable solution*. But it was to be Chip who would offer up yet another bombshell. He was really enjoying this.

"Hey, Boss. I guess we could ration the staples."

Shrieks, gasps, and a few expletives.

"Is he serious?" they whispered. "He's joking! He's not joking!" someone yelled out.

One poor soul groaned "I like my stapler!" Someone else let out a half-hearted 'I second' like this was a parliamentary procedure with votes and quorums.

The man who did the seconding had feeling in his voice but lacked sufficient bass to carry the day, so it sounded more like a plea than a statement. His 15 minutes of fame had been condensed to five seconds. That was all he would get – the famous seconder who tried to keep everyone's stapler. All eyes went from the 'I second' guy quickly to the boss.

Peter knew Chip's second idea was the one that would carry the day. Chip knew it too. If he had started out with the stapler plan it wouldn't have carried. Chip needed something extreme to soften the crowd up – cutting the air-conditioning elicited the right response and set the right conditions.

Peter, on the other hand, was conflicted. He didn't know how he was going to sell reduced staples to management as the fourth-floor's answer to budget cuts. Seemed petty and not terribly impactful. He had no choice.

There was an audible sigh from Peter, followed by slumped shoulders and the lowering of eyes. So much for his big debut. His assistant had already left.

"Go on," Peter said dejectedly and now utterly alone.

Part 1
Getting by and Getting Over

Chapter 1
Early May

When management rolled out their latest round of corporate initiatives hoping to improve morale, attract new talent, and grow the company, Chip Clementine looked skyward, pressed down hard on his asthma inhaler, and went to his happy place.

Chip had been in the workforce long enough to know what would come next – offsite retreats and forced social interactions in small rooms, talking about things that made him squirm in his seat.

He knew that after the talking and a few awkward confessions, there would be calls for the dreaded group hug. Chip didn't do hugs, didn't do validation. Apparently, everyone else did.

It was all too much for someone like Chip who fiercely guarded his privacy and avoided physical contact with anyone and anything. Chip actively avoided being in situations where the needy and desperate could share whatever it was on their mind. Chip was not all that interested in hearing about others and their needs. Having to listen to others was exhausting. People exhausted Chip.

At these corporate venues, there were heavy doses of management-speak with catchy buzzwords and bolded acronyms printed on glossy brochures and animated across projection screens. All would be expected to embrace the new company dogma and slogans.

But we're talking accountants and accountants do not so easily bend and sway with corporate fads and fashions, however splashy on the screen or on print.

Accountants, like Chip Clementine, despite a built-in aversion to change, would be recruited for a host of outdoor excursions, rope climbs, and the well-known trust-building exercises involving falling backward into the arms of co-workers, most of whom were not accountants and therefore couldn't be trusted.

Accountants trusted no one else in their company unless they were credentialed number crunchers of the highest order. It's just the way it is with accountants.

Corporate-driven events involved everything Chip despised because they were attempts to force people who rarely worked together to build more social, connective tissue with each other. For an accountant like Chip, building social connective tissue with anyone blurred many lines and was to be avoided at all costs.

These latest corporate announcements threatened to encroach on Chip's carefully balanced and constructed work life, but he would be ready for them. Chip tightened his grip on his asthma inhaler. A second inhale was moments away.

And then he remembered someone he knew who he could count on if times got tough, times, just like this, when pressure to join in on the corporate mantras and bandwagons would be intense. That's when Chip thought of his best friend, Bill.

Bill had been by Chip's side since Chip's first day on the fourth-floor, almost twenty years ago. Bill routinely saved Chip from pointless meetings, awkward social events, needy co-workers, and extra work on so many occasions and all because Bill knew exactly what to say and when to say it.

It took real talent, but Bill was the master of not saying anything at all when the situation called for it, and there were many times in Chip's world when the situation did indeed call for it. However, Bill wasn't human.

Bill was a desk accessory that Chip bought on the web for $19.95, plus shipping and handling.

Bill, for all of his redeeming qualities, was a battery-operated device. When Chip pushed Bill's button, a large, red button in the center of the device, Bill emitted pre-programmed, randomly selected messages designed specifically for Chip's needs – some light entertainment at another's expense.

Although some would regard Chip's best friend as nothing more than a gimmick, Chip had complete confidence in Bill's abilities and trusted him implicitly, especially when speaking with customers on the phone, when he volunteered to help out the folks in the call center.

Even though Chip was a die-hard accountant and shouldn't have been anywhere near actual customers, the call-center staff needed relief from time to time because they got pretty burned out.

So, arrangements had been made last year by management to offer incentives for those in other departments like Accounting, Purchasing, Human Resources, etc., who would volunteer for a shift or two from time to time. Chip was more than happy to volunteer if only to get out of more than one corporate retreat.

On such occasions, Bill was the perfect answer for Chip. When the requests to attend the latest corporate offsite came down, Chip was quick to mention to his supervisor that he had volunteered that week to help out folks in the call center. Chip was given a pass.

With the customer calls, Bill would be doing most of the work. Bill, not Chip, would be the one interacting with live, usually irate customers when they called into Chip's dedicated line to complain about the company's products.

Getting out of an offsite as well as getting some light entertainment would have been enough reason for everyone else to sign up and volunteer, but Chip was not everyone else. Chip saw volunteering as a means to a more lucrative end entirely. Volunteering helped his case each year when the dreaded performance evaluations were held and bonuses were paid out.

Since Chip usually struggled to articulate what he'd done all year, he could count on his volunteering time to fill in the blank space on the accomplishments section of his evaluation. *Volunteering was always a good filler*, Chip thought.

Volunteering ticked a few boxes for Chip; the first box being financial, the second one being comic relief. Volunteering for the sake of volunteering was a distant third. Volunteering did get Chip a few other bennies.

The bennies weren't much, but they were something. If you consistently volunteered, you got upgraded parking privileges for the following month. Upgraded parking gave him a little more gravitas around the fourth-floor breakroom when there was a lull in the conversation and someone needed to say something interesting.

Accountants, not really being known for saying anything interesting, would perk up if someone had snagged upgraded parking like hyenas would perk up if they saw something of interest from, say, across an African plain.

There were plenty of lulls in the breakroom because accountants were extreme introverts, so something had to be pretty dramatic for eyebrows to raise and for words to be spoken, even if in soft tones.

The breakroom was a complicated place to navigate for those that crunched numbers all day, confined to their cubicles and their spreadsheets and slaves to the coffee bean. The breakroom was a place where you went to have just enough interaction to tick the minimum social-interaction box to get your coffee refill.

Accountants preferred not to speak to other people but knew there was a certain expectation amongst each other that some superfluous discourse during the day was necessary. It didn't have to be much – refilling a coffee cup and a quick greeting (no eye contact though) would be sufficient.

Chip was a middle-of-the-road introvert but could play a slight extrovert on television if given the chance. He prided himself on crossing over between introvert and extrovert if the occasion demanded it. Before he made his twice-daily trip to fill up his coffee mug, he had his go-to greeting and a backup conversation starter if someone answered back.

He rarely needed a second backup conversation starter in the breakroom since a reply back to one of his standard greetings was usually met more by gesture than sound.

Chip didn't mind the economy of words, the muted gestures – it was the quiet professionalism that he liked the most about the fourth-floor. They all wore their badges of honor – degreed accountants with a common love for numbers, less love for humanity. Humanity talked too much.

So, when Chip, armed with a fresh cup of coffee, returned to his cubicle to start a voluntary call-center shift, after an exchange of the most minimum of pleasantries with some co-workers, Bill was nearby, charged up, and ready to go. All that now remained was for Chip to answer the phone and for Bill to step in.

The customer calls typically went like this.

Phone rings…Chip answers.

"Hi. You have reached Chip Clementine. Who am I speaking with?"

Customer: "This is (fill in the blank name) and I have a problem with the following product (fill in the product name)."

The customer then spends, on average, the next 48.5 seconds expanding on why he or she had the problem. Chip had timed them all while playing with his upgraded parking-pass lanyard. His lanyard was everything in these situations.

Chip places his headset mic next to Bill, presses Bill's big, red button, and waits in suspense as to which one of seven randomly produced phrases respond to the customer.

There are seven recordings, anyone of which would usually make Chip giggle and steady himself in his swivel chair to avoid another embarrassing fall.

Recording #1: "Sorry, would you say your name again?" There is a three-second pause then...

"Please spell it phonetically as I've recently learned the English language." This recording is repeated twice, usually while the customer is in the middle of phonetically spelling their name. The extended timing of the recording is designed to make the customer think Chip has difficulty with the English language. Chip doesn't have difficulty with English and nor does Bill, although Bill was made in China. The phone line is disconnected manually by Chip.

Recording #2: "That sounds awful – what a time you are having! Please elaborate further – I feel you're not telling me everything." Another timed pause then...

"I'm right here and not going anywhere." After 45 seconds, while presumably the customer is telling the inanimate, non-feeling Bill what is ailing them, Recording #3 kicks in whether the customer has finished speaking or not. The phone line is disconnected manually by Chip.

Recording #3: "I think you have the wrong number. Would you try calling back and see if I pick up, then we'll know you've reached the right number." The phone line is disconnected manually by Chip.

Recording #4: "I know exactly what you're going through. Would you like to speak to someone who can better address your concerns?" The line stays active until they hang up...hang up time varies...really varies.

Recording #5: "My apologies, but this is an internal line and not set up for customer service. Please hang up and visit our website for potential troubleshooting tips." The phone line disconnected manually by Chip.

Recording #6: "Unfortunately, I just started today and should really be attending my orientation. Please call back next week – I should be done by then." After 15 seconds, Recording #1 plays. The phone line is disconnected manually by Chip.

Recording #7: "I know this may sound silly, but do you think this may have something to do with your family medical history? You don't? Why not?" Programmed to pause for ten seconds then "I beg to differ. What about your grandfather?" Phone line is disconnected manually by Chip.

Bill was a godsend. He really was. If Bill did nothing else, he provided some levity under otherwise-stressful conditions, especially for an accountant who rarely, if ever, spoke with actual customers.

Chip refused to rank order which one of the recordings was his favorite – he wasn't going to go there. He wanted to experience the thrill of unscripted human interaction each time it happened without a safety net.

Bill always delivered. If Bill wasn't inanimate and could feel things, he would undoubtedly say that he found Chip slightly comical, especially while Bill was handling the customer. But Bill wasn't human and didn't feel anything for Chip or for the customer.

Chip never knew what type of customer he was going to get, or rather what kind of customer Bill was going to get, and he never knew what would come out of Bill's 'mouth.' Chip liked it that way for now. So did Bill. And with AAA batteries, he had a friend for life in Bill.

***

In addition to announcing their recent round of corporate initiatives, management decided to relax some of their long-standing policies. These particular policies dealt with prohibited activities in the workplace such as soliciting donations or selling things like popcorn, cookies, or other types of trinkets for either personal gain or for some community cause or organization.

All of that was out the window. Now, it was a free-for-all. Management in one email declared open season on all of the above. The email was pretty clear.

In their efforts to encourage greater community 'connection,' Chip read with increasing dread: Girl Scout cookie drives, among other things, was now allowed. Go Girl Scouts!

As he read that part of the email, Chip sharpened the last of his red pencils and braced for what he knew would come next – Mirriam. He didn't have to wait long.

Chip looked down the hallway and wasn't surprised to see Mirriam 30 feet out and fast approaching. She'd read the same email and was making a beeline for Chip.

Mirriam was intense, unrelenting. She took the intensity to another level. One would think that her daily 5 a.m. 'Extreme Body Pump' class with other equally charged suburban moms would take away some of her built-in stress and ground her emotionally when she came to work. It didn't, quite the opposite.

Her early morning workout fed her competitive drive and sustained her throughout the day, except when she felt a definite lull around 11 a.m. and then the power smoothie was only an arm's length way, staring at her, daring her to drink it all in one long gulp. She did, especially when someone was looking.

And with this day, Mirriam was free to canvas and sell Girl Scout cookies for her daughter's Girl Scout troop to a whole new selling market, as in Chip and the rest of the accountants on the fourth-floor. It was game on and game day all at once.

In reality, Mirriam was the one, more than her daughter, who was fully invested in those popular cookies. Mirriam's daughter, Madeline, had not wanted to be a girl scout, let alone wear a uniform or sell 'stupid' cookie boxes. This had all come out one night with her mom over takeout sushi.

Madeline had been managed her whole life – first with ballet, then with piano, and now with the Girl Scouts. She did what she was told because that's what you did with an overbearing, oppressive mother.

Secretly, Madeline held out a hope that this time, if she was able to make her cookie-sales goal, she could finish out her year, perhaps her final year, with the Girl Scout Troop and move onto other things, fun things with her friends, none of whom were in Girl Scouts.

In other times, Mirriam and Madeline would canvass her neighborhood, her church congregation, anyone in sight really except at work. Now, Mirriam had an entirely new line of prospects – her co-workers. Chip was an easy target.

Chip lived in her neighborhood and had been able to dodge most times she tried to sign him up for cookies. Last year, like most times, he didn't return the voicemails she left or the post-it notes left on his front door.

Back at work and in his cubicle, Chip knew how this was going to go down and started to shake, minor tremors really and mostly in the lower extremities. The shakes started with his legs, then made it to his arms and then to his ears, the final destination for all stress traffic in Chip's body. Yes, those ears were twitching by the time she invaded his personal space.

Mirriam had penetrating eyes and no body fat. Maybe some, but it was on borrowed time. She didn't do small talk, always leaned forward, and never slouched.

Enunciating every word so she wouldn't have to repeat herself, with eyebrows raised, she looked at Chip with that intensity and asked if she could count on him to sign up for 'some' Girl Scout cookies. The inference was clear. Sign up now, not later.

The word 'some' was deliberate. Someone like Mirriam defined what that 'some' would be for others. She had prefilled in the amount she wanted Chip to finance, another signature Mirriam move.

Chip was still in an elevated state. If human ears could flap, Chip thought, he would be elevated a couple of inches above his chair. He was cornered. There was no escape route, no easy exit, not even to the breakroom. This interaction would have to begin and end without artificial or chemical supports. He hoped Mrs. Clementine had put cash in his wallet recently. It would be needed.

The ear twitching or flapping, depending on one's political views, wouldn't stop.

He knew how to make it stop but it would likely cost him north of forty dollars. That's how much he paid for cookies that he didn't like the last time she successfully cornered him at their neighborhood cookout which was supposed to be stress-free and cordial.

Mirriam's goal was simple that morning. Get the money and move onto the next target/co-worker before one of the other ladies did (her competition). Forty dollars would put Chip in the clear. No checks, only cash. That's how much freedom cost.

She would wait at his cubicle until he returned from the ATM in the cafeteria, if necessary. He had her pick the type of cookies – he didn't care what they were, he wouldn't eat them anyway. He hated those cookies – bland, tasteless, and too many bright, wild colors.

Madeline hated them too, but they were a means to an end, and her mom, for all of her faults, was helping her get her ambitious quota.

Chip preferred conservative strands of gray and black, maybe some navy blue. Chip wasn't proud of himself, but some things like Mirriam's quest for cookie sales were better handled with cash. It was cleaner somehow.

He surmised early on that his only victory over her would be paying her what she wanted slowly in cash with one-dollar bills.

That was his only solace, his only defense. Mrs. Clementine, thankfully, had put Chip's weekly cash allowance in his wallet that morning. He would blow all of it on Mirriam, her daughter, and those cookies.

Mrs. Clementine always gave Chip his allowance for the week and it was always in one-dollar bills like, somehow, one-dollar bills would slow Chip's spending habits. This was not the only passive-aggressive move in their marriage.

Mirriam's annoyance at having to watch Chip slowly stuff the one-dollar bills into her donation envelope was the only victory he could gain from all of this.

It was over before it began. Chip secured his freedom from her for a cost of eight overpriced boxes of Girl Scout cookies he would never eat.

The exchange of cash and seeing Mirriam dashing off to the next unsuspecting accountant was what Chip needed to get all his bodily functions back in balance. Maybe next year he could resist her?

Where were his friends when he needed them?

That was easy. They had given him and her plenty of space when they saw Mirriam before Chip did, choosing to watch that encounter from the breakroom like the sheep that they were.

Looking back over those past couple of weeks, Chip was feeling quite proud of himself. He had avoided being swept up and calendared into the first couple of corporate off-sites and his volunteering gig was still safe and secure and serving more than one purpose. The real curveball had been Mirriam, but he had navigated out of that without too much scar tissue.

Chip was a survivor – he would do what he needed to do to get by and get over whenever and wherever possible, and no one did it better than Chip on the fourth-floor.

Chip was also a pretty good accountant but he was an even better corporate player – managing the ups, downs, and sideways that kept him well in control and below the radar.

As May goes, this was all pretty standard fare for Chip Clementine, but this was a leap year, and he was sure there was more drama and excitement left in the month.

He was right.

Chapter 2

More of May and Almost June

The corporate initiatives announced earlier in the month didn't end with advertisements for off-sites and retreats, nor did it end with the opening up of fund drives and cookie sales in the office.

Not wanting to be outdone by far more famous companies than theirs, management decided to go all out at its headquarters with a new line of décor that they hoped would send the right messages to its workforce, mostly to the ones they wanted to keep. The company was getting a bit of reputation in the valley and it was not a good one.

Year after year, the company was missing the mark in its attempts to recruit young workers into the ranks. To those that took note of these things, it was no secret that there were far too many on payroll averaging in the forties and fifties, close to their retirement years.

The company needed a younger, more diverse infusion of human capital. They needed more hip, more spunk, less gray, and more confident colors in their ranks.

Thus, the rollout of hardware, furniture, and bling had to be impressive and appealing to the younger crowd in the company's employ but also to future recruits from a demographic of which they were most definitely in short supply.

There was new carpet, upgraded countertops in the bathrooms, and see-through refrigerators in all the breakrooms. But it didn't stop there. A jungle-themed tree house was installed in the atrium as well as an eighties video arcade in the cafeteria.

No less than six meditation rooms (with mood lighting), one for each of the six floors in the building, were configured overnight by converting excess-storage rooms – excess for some, but not for others. Meditation rooms came with padded, soundproof walls, fresh stocks of incense, plenty of beads, and a stereo system with iPhone jacks for the surround. Someone on the management team was clearly a meditation-room guru.

Last but not least, there were 'napping chairs' or pods, as the younger crowd called them. These pods, installed on every floor, were high-end, hard plastic-encased relaxation chairs that advertised uninterrupted napping time to those that needed a break from the daily grind. It was the latest craze and management was eager to keep up with the latest fads.

The pods, more than any other corporate initiative, generated the most interest. Many found excuses to walk by the pods, slowing down to stare at the odd-shaped, sci-fi-looking chairs.

Management told the staff that the pods were available for thirty minute napping increments, giving people a time and a space to rewind, recharge, and recuperate. All you had to do was sign up for your nap time for that day and you were all set.

It was all very exciting for the exactly the younger demographic the company was targeting; the older crowd not so much. They were quick to label the pod initiative part of a broader corporate agenda to push employees and the rest of America into a surveillance state. What would happen next, they wondered out loud. Uniforms? Voluntary gene testing? Two-hour lunch breaks?

The older accountants on the fourth floor, like Chip Clementine, conceded grudgingly that this latest initiative was 'legit' because the flyer advertising the pod was a) in color, and b) laminated, and c) posted in the breakroom for maximum exposure.

Even management had thought in their wisdom that accountants could use a nap every once in a while, which was a little surprising since accountants were generally left alone unless something really boring had to be discussed in a meeting or someone needed an equally boring report that only the accountants knew how to produce for them. Then someone would call for them.

But until then, they were happy to stay in the cubicles and crunch numbers all day long. The fourth-floor was the quietest floor in the building – no other floor came close.

Most of the accountants were younger than Chip, and quite a few of them were Zoomers, officially known as Generation Z, determined to claim their place as the next spoiled, entitled, and privileged generation. The Zoomers already knew what a pod was and what it offered them. They didn't need to be educated or enticed. Some of their friends worked at other companies that already had these pods and they were quite jealous. They were hopeful that something like this would come sooner or later.

Now that the pods had arrived, it didn't take long for them to give their ringing endorsement with donated fresh fruit, some Middle Eastern throw rugs placed around the pod, and burning incense sticks, all of which reminded Chip of days gone by, lost forever.

But where most saw the seductive pods as an excuse to catch a nap, Chip, as one of the more devious old-timers, saw them as something completely different – a way to settle old scores and past grievances. He would have some harmless fun at someone else's expense.

His mind began to race but not too hard. The rising heartburn was an informal but effective way to gauge his stress level when things got a little excitable. However, on this occasion, the heartburn was due less to the excitement and more to the spicy Mexican lunch he had wolfed down too fast at his cubicle.

Now, in his post-lunch, lethargic state, Chip tried to fight off his fatigue and concentrate on how he could capitalize on this nap-pod contraption.

Chip did some deep breathing, focusing on the present. Some would say his breathing techniques were a nod to the mindfulness craze, and to some degree it was, but Chip wasn't trying to relax; he was trying to scheme with real intent. Scheming took energy and carbs.

Within moments, Chip had sorted out his thoughts and come to one clear conclusion – these pods, like other gadgets, would require a level of human supervision, and with supervision came power. With power, Chip smirked with his eyes closed, came opportunity.

Chip didn't want his line of reasoning to end there. He smirked some more. One of his cubicle neighbors was eyeing him and thought it odd that anyone practicing mindfulness would smirk.

Heather never smirked when she tried to relax and so why would anyone else, she wondered. Heather also wondered if things would have been quieter in her workday if she had chosen to be a librarian instead of an accountant.

This was an ongoing battle she waged with herself. Some days, accountant; other days, librarian. Spreadsheets over books or books over spreadsheets.

Some days she hated her job and thought about libraries and how people would go to libraries and check out books and could read at their leisure pretty much all day. *Anymore smirking*, she thought, *and the tilt toward librarian might not be able to be reversed.*

These are some of the things frustrated accountants thought about while sitting in there. Heather sighed quietly and then went back to reviewing another mindlessly boring financial report that no one would read because it wasn't intuitive and was easy to delete when it came through as an email attachment.

Meanwhile, Chip continued to smirk. *There would be many who would sign up for their pod time*, he thought. Someone had to inject order into, what would likely be, a hot mess of heated arguments over preferred naptime slots, etc. Someone had to be the leader here, or at least that was Chip's cover. And, who better to raise their hand and volunteer than one of the more senior, experienced staff?

Chip mouthed the words silently after his rhetorical question – 'meeeeeee,' and let the word linger for a while. He liked saying the word 'me'; it felt liberating, self-affirming, not selfish, but liberating.

The wannabe librarian shushed Chip loudly, but he ignored her. It wasn't the first time he had been shushed by a fellow accountant and it wouldn't be his last.

He was no leader, Chip thought, but he'd put his time in over the years and the others looked up to him, especially when an intermediary, even a broker of sorts, was needed between management and the 'worker bees.' That was the public reason, Chip thought, for volunteering his name to be arbiter of all things pod-wise.

He would speak to management and 'selflessly' volunteer to manage the access, the signups, the schedule, the priority – all of it.

Chip opened his eyes and told himself to stop smiling. His next stop was Jeffrey, his manager, and decision authority on all things on the fourth-floor. Chip would explain to him how this pod initiative would backfire if not properly managed...by, of course, Chip. Jeffrey's door was open so Chip walked in and closed the door.

Chip was careful to paint an apocalyptic picture with big words and a couple of whiteboard drawings. Jeffrey was annoyed that Chip would interrupt him so quickly after his lunch was over, but big animal pictures had a way of settling him down and reminding him of simpler times.

Jeffrey didn't like to do anything until his body had fully adjusted from his lunch and it hadn't adjusted. He was feeling a little too full and a little bit grumpy. Chip would have to tread carefully.

Chip conjured up images of otherwise pleasant, passive, and sedentary employees switching to keyed up, twitchy, and paranoid as they fought over coveted pod timeslots in a world without order, Chip's order that is.

Jeffrey was easily startled as Chip conjured up one chaotic fourth floor scene after another. Jeffrey saw the beauty and logic of Chip's argument right away but missed entirely Chip's underlying motive. And when Jeffrey was startled coupled with impressed, he easily gave in.

With a flick of the hand and a nod, Chip had gotten what he wanted – authority combined with access. *In the arena of life, Jeffrey was a spectator, standing squarely on the sidelines*, Chip thought.

Jeffrey handed over the pod user manual and gave Chip the system administrator password with a handshake and a wink that didn't look natural.

Chip now had authority and access to go in the backdoor, so to speak, and manually schedule and adjust all requests from his own computer without anyone noticing or suspecting. Thanks, Jeffrey!

After a few minutes on his computer, accessing the pod system, Chip realized he could do other things with the pod. He could program the chair's movements – direction, speed, height, you name it. Oh yes, Chip thought, this was going to be fun and (if played well) non-attributional.

He would settle old scores and address past grievances all through his pod. Past grievances had three names – William, Ted, and LaTisha.

Each had offended Chip in some way, mostly unintentionally but nonetheless worthy of payback. The punishment would fit the crime.

He would start with William.

Chip never liked the name William. Chip knew he had his quirks and one of them was making snap judgments of people purely because of their name, like William.

He knew he was arbitrary and flip but thought anyone named William was born into this world pious and left or right of center (he didn't care). William's time in the pod, Chip promised himself, would be fun and exhilarating for all the wrong reasons.

And then there was Ted, poor Ted.

His crime was speaking far too long during a staff meeting. Chip kept track of any that was the reason why meetings went over, and Ted's name had been recorded on Chip's 'blotter' more than once. Ted was a repeat offender. But the meeting that got Ted elevated from blotter to Chip's special 'pod list' was last Wednesday.

In another boring staff meeting with no agenda, Jeffrey had droned onto everyone about the importance of not wasting office supplies (staples in particular), and Ted made it a point to challenge the use of staples versus going with binder clips. Chip was a stapler guy through and through – had been all his life.

Ted passionately argued for everyone to use binder clips instead of staples over environmental concerns. His impassioned plea for abandonment of all-things staplish in favor of binder clips drew support from the quiet ones in the group, which was most of the group since they were accountants.

The meeting had run over by twenty-eight minutes. That was actually the more telling point than whether staples or binder clips were involved.

When the meeting ended, Chip had ten minutes (rather than two hours) to decompress before leaving for the day. Ted had committed the sin of infringing on Chip's end-of-day routine and, for that, had secured his spot on Chip's list. There was no coming back from that faux-pas.

And then there was LaTisha to round out the list.

Last year, Chip and Russell, another aging accountant, were discussing an upcoming Star Trek convention, dressed in their Trekkie costumes. Things went sideways when they started to pick apart each other's costumes, arguing that theirs was better than the others – finer materials and more realistic, etc.

LaTisha couldn't contain herself and burst out laughing when they started to wrestle near Chip's cubicle. The sight of a Klingon and a Cardassian was too much for her. Her shrill laughter stopped the mayhem as both looked up to see her almost in tears; she was laughing so hard. Chip had never felt more vulnerable in a Klingon uniform, even with his ray gun.

What LaTisha didn't realize is that no one laughs at Trekkies in their official uniforms/costumes. Outsiders, according to the rules, hadn't earned the right to weigh-in on these official matters, especially convention garb.

One year on and Chip had not forgotten LaTisha, and so she was the last one to round out his special nap pod list. LaTisha's experience with the pod chair, like Ted's, would be quite different from what she was expecting.

The list was complete – William, Ted, and LaTisha. After studying the pod manual, all Chip could do was wait, hope and pray for each one to sign up for this experimental pod experience.

Once they logged into the pod portal, he could work his scheduling and programming magic.

***

When the email from Jeffrey came out, all three were quick to sign up online for their thirty minutes. From his cubicle, and with system access, Chip tracked who signed up and for what time slot. As Chip scanned the electronic roster, a slight smile flashed across his aging face as he saw all three had signed up for later that day. Fortunately, he had planned his little tricks already.

He felt like a kid on Christmas morning, the first to go downstairs and see all the presents. It looked like William would be the first one up.

For William's pod experience, William would think he was getting his thirty minutes, but his time would be cut short.

He would be woken by the activation of a sound feature in the pod, one minute early, with a combination of police sirens and the office's repeating emergency evacuation alarm. Chip had modified the pod's default sound settings to suit his purposes.

These sounds were not regular options for pod participants, but Chip found a way to work a few sound files of his own into the system! Chip was hoping that William would put on a good show for the rest of the floor when he exited the pod in, what Chip hoped would be, a combination of shock and bewilderment. William would not disappoint.

For Ted, Chip thought some stock-standard water torture wouldn't be so bad. Chip would let Ted nap only for ten minutes and then slowly bring him out of slumber with slow-dripping water from a hidden tube that connected the pod to the nearby men's bathroom.

If done right, the water would trickle through the top of the pod and onto Ted's exposed forehead. There was a method to Chip's madness.

The drops were not large enough to trigger a machine malfunction but small enough to cause irritation and mild concern as Ted would near the end of his slumber. Chip wasn't a sleep specialist but remained hopeful that the drip-drip of the water would somehow make it into Ted's REM state.

Chip also hoped that Ted's dreams would be altered accordingly involving water. But that was a stretch.

For LaTisha, there would be no mercy.

The pod that she occupied would be programmed by Chip to rotate and elevate several feet above the ground while she was off in her own 'la-la' land. Apparently, pod chairs had been used by the aviation industry as pseudo flight simulators in a past life and some of these features hadn't been disabled.

Her wake-up call would be live-streamed on YouTube, capturing the change in facial expressions from sweet slumber to sheer terror as she was unceremoniously dropped ten feet onto carefully placed exercise mats, borrowed from the meditation rooms.

The stage was set. Chip had the will, a wrench, an energy bar, and an iPhone handy. He was a little nervous. This was more complicated than most of the other pranks he did from time to time. He knew the masses would be entertained only for so long before getting bored and going back to building some PowerPoint slides.

A lot was riding on this. But it had to go down without anything pointing back to him. There couldn't be an audit trail.

Chip had a chequered past with office pranks. He still carried the weight of the last one on his shoulders that had misfired, literally, since it involved fireworks and way too much smoke for the fire detectors to handle. This one would be different.

No one, he hoped, would know that Chip was behind this. He would tell no one, except a close confidant, of his deeds. Timing was everything, and it went exactly to plan.

William was the first one in the pod out of the three. With the jerry-rigged video recording everything inside, Chip waited to see if his reprogramming of William's pod experience would play out the way he hoped. It did. Ten minutes in and William had drifted away.

Chip could tell William was out cold by a jerry-rigged audio line into the pod. He could hear the light snoring.

At minute marker twenty-nine, the audio kicked in violently, waking William with a jolt. Chip could see William was clearly panicked and a little disoriented.

Chip disabled the door inside the pod for such an occasion, and William's attempts to open the pod from the inside, as well as the grunts, yelps, and low-grade profanity were live-streamed across the fourth-floor on the hallway monitors usually reserved for updated stock-market reports.

Of course, this didn't stop onlookers from capturing the experience on their smartphones and comparing shooting angles during multiple playbacks amongst themselves afterward. The episode lasted thirty seconds, but for William, it was an eternity.

Although not fully awake when the door lock was finally released and he fell out onto the padded floor, he had taken it in stride and carried on bravely with a slight eye twitch which ended up lasting for a couple of weeks.

To add salt to the wound, William's episode picked up some traction on other social-media sites. William became somewhat of a reluctant celebrity throughout the building. But the unwanted attention forced William deeper and deeper into his shell.

His friends would later say that it was about that time he started to consider a new line of work, one that involved getting back to nature and long walks alone, maybe zoo-keeping or wildlife-ranger work.

William thought the pod had malfunctioned and never dreamed there had been foul play.

Ted was next and walked into the pod, wondering what all the fuss was about, having seen William walking out a little dazed and wet! Ted was no stranger to all things like napping chairs or deep recliners for that matter. He passed through Bangkok a few years ago and availed himself of what the city offered, involving plenty of comfortable chairs, dark rooms, and incense sticks.

Ted considered himself an adopted son of mainland Asia despite being very, very white. To him, the pod was an extension of the Asian life he always wanted. This would complete him, he thought, maybe even make him feel more comfortable in his new job at a new company.

But, thanks to Chip, Ted would not be traveling back to Thailand that day.

Chip's make-do water tube had been placed in the pod for one reason and one reason only – to provide a few seconds of enjoyment without inflicting long-lasting mental damage. Unfortunately, this one went a bit too far.

At the appointed time, and with the press of a button from the safety and security of Chip's cubicle, water began to drip on Ted's forehead.

The first few drops triggered childhood trauma. What Chip couldn't have known is that Ted, as a boy, was locked in a closet by his older brother near a leaky toilet that had drip-dripped for a couple of lonely hours before his mom had found him.

Chip knew that playing with dripping water on another person's head was pushing things a little, so the treatment only lasted for a minute, but it was enough to wake Ted up and beg to be let out.

Ted left the pod with the aid of others, more for emotional support than anything else. He would get over this, at least that is what his mom told him the following day over a warm soup and homemade bread.

Later, he would tell anyone who would listen how he never understood how a nap pod could leak! The others would smile empathetically but still worry about him.

LaTisha's special treatment involved more acrobatics.

Her ten-foot vertical drop from the nap pod was spectacular, more for what came out of her mouth than anything else. The terror on her face matched her high-pitched, guttural scream that ended with a rough landing.

After the fall and then a few seconds collecting herself off of the floor mats, LaTisha sprinted from the scene with handbag flapping in the wind.

Chip wasn't a mean, conniving person. He did his share of good deeds, but they were usually conditioned on something or someone that would benefit him in the short or long term; he wasn't picky. He kept scores and tallies, actually more tallies than scores, and he knew he was an imperfect being, prone to snap judgments and false assumptions.

Those in his circle thought he had gone too far but laughed nervously anyway. Still, Chip was, if nothing else, a capitalist and not above offering similar services to others interested in their own form of payback...but for a price.

The nap pods were now tainted goods, but he was willing to look elsewhere in the building to set his traps, so to speak. His currency was food, and his price was donuts, but only a certain kind.

For a half-dozen of those chocolate-covered, custard-filled delights, he would hold court around his cubicle and consider such requests from anyone with a grievance, however petty, with another.

The donuts got you the sit-down meeting but did not seal the deal. Those who had known Chip for years considered him discrete and professional, but a snob when it came to donuts. He had standards.

Chip was not an easy read. He was complicated. May had come and gone, but June was next, and Chip didn't know if he could handle two Mays in a row. In the safety of his cubicle, Chip downed a nearby, half-empty (he was a half-empty guy) Diet Coke and thought about June.

He spent a lot of time, too much time, thinking about how things impacted him and less about how they impacted others. He was self-aware enough to know this about himself, but nothing seismic enough had happened in his life for him to consider changing, at least not yet.

Chapter 3

Cash Cows and Other Sacred Rituals

With June came flowers and metaphors of renewal, rebirth, and change, but none of that sat very well with Chip. Chip liked to keep things just the way they were. Change was, and always would be, overrated.

To resist change, Chip spent his life creating personal space, defining his rules, and setting safe boundaries. He built a carefully constructed persona at work, one that kept people in check, managers at a distance, and his inner circle secure.

To overcome his natural anxieties of being around people, he employed control mechanisms, some that gave him emotional cover but others that just made money – cold, hard cash, usually in one-dollar bills. Making money from a side hustle was a sure way to put his blood pressure down and his spirits high.

The small refrigerator under his desk was his latest venture. Who would have thought that this side-hustle, a mini-fridge of all things, would be the cash cow that would bankroll his annual pilgrimage to Orlando and the Magic Kingdom?

Chip would pinch himself occasionally on his good fortune but not too much and not too hard; soft tissue damage had a way of staying permanent in the most embarrassing of places.

The idea of renting his mini fridge out to co-workers was fairly straightforward. For the price of a dollar a week, Chip would store a beverage of their choice in his mini-fridge.

He didn't judge others by what they brought him – Pepsi versus Coke, etc. Although, anyone showing up with ginger ale was marked down with an asterisk…bolded if it was diet.

Chip dealt only in all-cash transactions sealed with a handshake. There were no contracts, no lawyers – just an understanding that if the cover was blown, it was everyone for themselves.

He knew he was probably violating some company policy but never bothered to ask. Plausible deniability, he realized, was not reserved for high-elected office! So, Chip never read any company policy. It was safer that way, somehow liberating not knowing exactly if he was out of line or not.

If he was called out for illegal profiteering on company time and things went south in a hurry, he had practiced his lines in case of such an event.

Management interventions were rare on the fourth-floor, but when they happened, they were loud and very public. Management usually had collected enough evidence of a discretion or two to ensure that things went down their way so why not make a spectacle of someone for good measure and make the manager look bold and decisive – it was a twofer, and twofers in a manager's world were like comets colliding in a good way. They didn't happen very often, but when they did, you might as well get it on camera.

Chip rehearsed this worst-case scenario in his mind dozens of times if and when he got caught making money on company time. He predicted how this would play out in the heat of the moment. It went something like this.

Chip acts surprised after being confronted by Peter, the manager of the day, on what appears to be the inappropriate use of a mini fridge under Chip's desk. Chip is quick to respond, even as the crowd gathers around Chip's cubicle area. "No, Peter, I don't hire out space in my mini-refrigerator for money." Chip would say this loudly so everyone watching could easily hear him.

In the early moments, the crowd could go either way, but they usually stuck around because there was usually nothing else remotely interesting going on at the moment.

Peter's shrill voice was at a distinct disadvantage to Chip's. Peter knew it and so did Chip, but each played the part. Chip was ready for Peter and his clipboard.

Next, Peter would say some 'Blah, Blah,' using management-speak (i.e., a few acronyms, some buzz words, and slightly raised tones when using words ending with 'ing'). Chip would respond.

"Yes, I know that no one else owns a mini-refrigerator and that there are plenty of normal refrigerators in the breakroom," Chip would say in a faked and resigned tone. There would be a pause for effect while waiting for the next inevitable question.

A little more blah, blah, blah from Peter choosing to interrogate Chip a little more. Chip would answer emphatically, "No, that isn't my Diet Coke in the mini-fridge. It actually is Bob's. I know it's Bob's."

Final 'Blah, Blah,' from Peter.

"Okay. It's a deal," Chip would say. "I won't take any more beverage-storage orders and you get to store your Salsa Tortilla Wraps – no charge, and no questions asked." Chip would say the last part quietly so only Peter could hear him because none of them wanted the crowd to hear that a deal had been struck.

Chip would feel the rush every time he got something over someone, although, this would be technically a win-win for both Peter and Chip since no credibility was lost on either side. From a distance, Peter would look like he was in charge and Chip would look like he had been caught.

Chip knew, despite the optics, he would still come out of it flush with a stash of crumpled dollar bills in his middle drawer. Chip was living large and amply rewarded for services provided. He was a capitalist, a tradesman. Not everyone can ride business class, he reasoned.

And not everyone can afford to drive 14 hours to Disney whenever they want, strap on Mickey's ears, and enjoy priority-line passes.

***

Some days, though, were not so stellar. Chip's job was fairly routine, and mundane but it still wore on him from time to time. On those days, when it seemed everything was heading downhill fast, he would look to other people to give him the lift he needed to finish out his day on a high note, people like the department's newest hire, Justin.

Justin's misfortune, at least until someone else was hired, was to be assigned the least desirable cubicle in the office, the one closest to the printer used heavily by Chip and the more senior accountants on the floor.

That cubicle went to the newest hire. Sitting in that cubicle for any length of time would subject the occupant to stressors and nuisances unique to that part of the office.

One could say it was a rite of passage and one Justin would have to pass through until the next newest hire came along and Justin would be bumped up to a new and better cubicle. It's just the way things worked on the fourth-floor.

Justin was no dummy. He'd been hired under the company's corporate internship program after successfully navigating six rounds of interviews.

Justin was offered a chance to go permanent after a successful rotation in the Accounting Department (i.e. the fourth-floor). But, like so many other Zoomers, he felt entitled and thought his initial cubicle assignment was simply 'sub-par' and not commensurate with his station in life – a newly minted and degreed accountant.

After orientation, Justin voiced his displeasure with his cubicle assignment in a way only someone from his generation could (a three-page email to his mentor filled with charged words, but mostly emojis of why he should sit somewhere else).

Justin complained, mostly with charged words and colorful imagery, that the local printer next to his cubicle was disturbing in its size and proximity to him.

It was unsightly (stained carpet), smelled (lingering pet odor from last 'bring your dog to work day'), and was everyone's dumping ground (think empty pizza boxes and stale Dorito chips from a recent 'whatev's day').

He said to his mentor that the printer affected his creativity and spark, an unusual thing to say since he was, by all measures, an accountant and, thus, born to be in short supply of creativity and spark.

If he was being honest, Justin felt the printer hunched over him, encroaching on his personal space. He needed his space to think and to thrive, he told himself. The printer was preventing him from thinking just by its very presence.

After all, he was a recent university graduate of a top-notch school with the whole world before him, or that is at least what his favorite professors had told him.

The printer – everyone called it 'The Beast' – was made decades ago and never been replaced; no one would dare. It was six feet long by four feet wide by four feet high, a massive technological triumph in its day.

It had a work ethic of sorts, however temperamental, working perfectly fine until noon and then embarking on a series of stops and starts at the most inconvenient times through to the early evening.

Most had given up and planned their printing times before lunch – no print job in the queue could be guaranteed to print after that time.

The Beast had its fair share of enemies, despite a cult following that grew over the years. Many an adoring fan or grudging admirer had taken selfies with The Beast. It really was a little much, Chip thought, but he didn't begrudge anyone their heroes, even if they were inanimate.

And so, Justin was forced into this cubicle-printer coexistence, knowing that every new hire did their time working in the shadows of The Beast.

They would be joined together until the next new hire showed up and the cubicle-assignment process would start anew, bumping Justin out and inserting someone new into the madness of the fourth-floor.

Justin was encouraged on most days with the mantra of 'this too shall pass.' He wasn't a religious person, but after a week, he did start to think of things in terms of black and white, good and evil.

He started to write fluorescent-colored post-it notes of popular verses from the Bible between him and the printer along the partitioned wall to give him strength and resiliency when he would get claustrophobic.

But, overall, the size, noise, and location of The Beast was not really the major issue.

The real issue, if he had enough time to think about it clearly, what with the heat and noise from the ceiling fan, was the number of unclaimed print jobs left on top of the printer that was piled up and tilted toward Justin's workspace. He surmised that many a printed report had been accidentally sent to The Beast and most had not bothered to collect and that was the problem.

After a certain number, the piled-up print jobs would eventually slide off the printer into Justin's ever-shrinking workspace. The slide of hundreds of individual paper sheets resembled a miniature white paper avalanche coming toward him.

Sometimes he would think about moving out of the way, but something in the back of his mind said the paper would find him anyway, so he just sat there and let the paper come to him just to get it over with.

Justin didn't mind random paper mounds crashing down all around him, but the paper cuts on his neck were a little much and he could only muffle his pain for so long.

It was like the paper knew where to attack Justin – repeatedly slicing the same neck area as if it was punishing him for joining the company and, even more, for deciding to pursue a career in accounting.

Justin knew this was a test of sorts; he just didn't know if he could see the light at the end of the tunnel.

Seeing Justin suffer provided just enough light entertainment for Chip to keep him powering through most afternoons with a renewed sense of purpose. Seeing Justin creatively stave off most (but not all) of the paper that cascaded onto him was even more inspiring.

How Justin managed to keep it together without walking out and seeking another credentialed profession was mystifying to Chip.

Still, even heroes have their moments of doubt. As Justin would curse from a particularly painful paper cut, Chip reasoned that everyone did their time in the trenches and Justin was no different. He'd been Justin once, heck, everyone had. He would get through this.

Almost everyone did.

Chip didn't want to think about what happened two new hires ago with Alicia. Her manager was still trying to figure out what went wrong and where to send her things (she hadn't bothered to come back and collect them).

Justin, to his credit, however, was surrounded by a strong network of family and friends, people willing to hear his stories and support him through most things. All of that helped him through the first week or two but not beyond. Everyone has a breaking point.

Justin hit his one late evening when, nursing several recent paper cuts from earlier in the day, he was asked to pull an overnighter to make a deadline that had come up too quickly and surprised everyone. Justin hit his 'wall.'

Paper cuts, the 'Beast,' the snickering from others, and now an overnighter. It was all too much. Justin couldn't function without nine hours of sleep or his body pillow.

Justin didn't hesitate – he only had so much to give and an overnighter was the last straw. He couldn't do this anymore.

He knew he had options and other departments would probably salivate over getting someone with accounting skills to help them out in a pinch.

Chip didn't begrudge Justin for requesting a transfer out of accounting. Chip, just like the others, did his time with The Beast, and asking Justin to pull an overnighter on the heels of so many paper cuts probably was a bridge too far for someone like Justin.

Chip granted the request and Justin transferred to Marketing where they were in high demand for someone with analytical skills.

Turns out, Marketing was a better fit for Justin.

They had modern copiers, open workspaces, and lots of snap celebrations each day for the most minor events, in Chip's opinion, like when someone finished a marketing plan, wanted to share a new recipe with co-workers or decided someone had gutted through a tough morning and needed group affirmation of their effort.

Someone still needed to help out on an overnighter and Chip, still being bored for most of that week up till then, thought why not.

Chip had pulled overnighters many times before and formed friendships with others that would last a lifetime.

***

The work-related reasons for pulling an overnighter were many – making a deadline, making up for missing a deadline, etc. But Chip liked the overnighters for what they really were – a glimpse into another's soul.

Nothing was more honest, more telling than to be in the moment with another human being at three in the morning, copying, collating, and stapling financial reports, interrupted by an occasional yelp from a paper cut or grunt from a staple jam.

Secrets, confidences, aspirations, and some over-the-top yarns were all shared freely without fear of reprisal, part of the unspoken rules that in the still of the night with neon lights illuminating a stark hallway; it's game on with blurred boundaries of behavior.

Unspoken rules and blurred boundaries reminded Chip of one of his more memorable overnighters from a few years ago.

Chip's stapler buddy for that particular overnighter was Mark. Mark had been recruited for the overnighter because there would be a lot of stapling and Mark was known around the floor as a stapler in a league all of his own. Chip was more of a collator than a stapler.

Mark's cubicle was three cubicles down and one row over, which was basically another country with a language, culture, and menu all of its own.

Chip sized Mark up when he had first joined the office (looks like a stapler guy than a collator guy) but, oh, how wrong he had been about Mark.

After only fifteen minutes of privileged conversation during their stapling/collating, Mark, Chip learned, was much more than an expert stapler.

Mark had climbed Everest, blindfolded, without guides.

Mark had run with the bulls in Pamplona. Technically, the bulls had run with him.

He survived a shark attack. The shark hadn't.

Mark spoke four languages but refused to speak three for reasons he wouldn't or couldn't disclose, at least not in words.

Chip had been so wrong about Mark. *There's so much we miss about someone when we work regular hours with them*, Chip thought.

Mark was exceptional and clearly an underachiever. He handled the stapler like it was an extension of his body. Why had he chosen to make his mark here, at this company, in this department, on this floor? Chip was perplexed.

As Mark continued in hushed tones describing some of his exploits, Chip had to remind himself to take breaths.

He never met anyone like Mark. He knew this was a harmless bromance and completely situationally dependent, but he couldn't help but compare himself to Mark.

Chip took comfort that, when he was younger, back in elementary school, he had proudly taken third place in a 'Mr. Muscle Man' competition at a local community center.

Later, during his early teenage years, he snorkeled in a dolphin-discovery cove which some might argue, especially Chip, was on par with some of Mark's exploits that pushed human limits.

To put this in context, Chip voluntarily entered the discovery cove despite being deathly afraid of seawater, sea animals – anything to do with water or currents or anything that moved through water...like dolphins.

Surely that counted for something, Chip thought. He had looked fear in the face, well, maybe a dolphin's face. Even though it looked like it was smiling at him, it was still unnerving behind the submerged glass cage while kids half his age looked on...on the other side of the cage with the dolphins.

He was practically Mark, Chip concluded, but with less chest hair and maybe an inch or two smaller in foot size.

Chip felt a kindred spirit in Mark. They formed a connection, a bond. He was sure there would be more conversations, more honesty. The stapling and collating continued unabated.

He knew there was another pair of accountants down the hallway doing the same thing, but it wasn't the same thing really.

In that hallway, in the still of the night and with the hum of the copier and the sound of manual stapling, Chip thought long and hard about whether to pursue scuba qualification at his local Y.M.C.A. and then maybe swim with the dolphins in the ocean like Mark would do.

***

The excitement of that overnighter with Mark was short-lived, however. Most of the satisfaction he enjoyed at work was in the dull and the routine, punctuated by daily lunchtime walks, allowing Chip to see things so clearly while others would struggle to make sense of it all.

His lunchtime walks formed the core of his personal fitness regime and, he thought, was a model for others to follow. If they would only listen.

He fervently wished he could bottle up his secrets of physical and mental wellbeing and sell it on Amazon, but he wasn't prepared for that kind of wealth, fame, and publicity, so he kept it to himself.

Going to the gym, signing up for classes, walking or jogging, and other well-known and documented forms of exercise involving sweating were for those that hadn't caught onto Chip's universal secret for being in top physical shape in the modern age – concentrated imagination.

Yes, by simply elevating one's mental powers, one could increase in physical resilience and strength. No sweating required and certainly no need for indoor or outdoor gyms. Chip's secret to physical health involved two parts. The first part involved a brisk walk around the corporate building three times each day – a total distance of four-hundred meters for a maximum walking time of fifteen minutes.

That was his warm-up and about as close as he would get to a rising body temperature.

He would then walk up the stairs back to his office, put a sign next to his cubicle that said '*Do not disturb – lunch break*,' put on his sunglasses, lean back, and start the most challenging part of his workout.

48

For the next twenty minutes (he had a timer), Chip would call upon all of his mental powers to imagine he was transported to the Amazon and the deep jungle with lots of heat, snakes, and no air-conditioning.

The whoops and shouts from the natives would be heard in the far-off distance (again, in his mind) as they pursued Chip toward the river, smelling their next meal.

Chip would run (imaginary run) as if his very life depended upon it, running up and down hills and valleys, jungles, and other types of terrain, attempting to outrun sweaty cannibals with big, white teeth and poisoned blow darts.

He knew this was what pure adrenalin felt like. He heard others talk about it. He could now relate to them. The adrenalin coursed through his body because the heartbeat counter on his Fitbit was a little above normal.

While everyone else in the office ate their microwaved lunch, Chip was in a virtual fight for his life, but not so much in a fight that he didn't raise his glasses every so often to check on his heart rate and stretch out his ankles when they hadn't moved in a while.

There were always close calls, but Chip somehow managed to keep it together, to stay alive (virtually) until the beeper on his wristwatch went off (vibrate mode) and he notched up another intense workout for the week.

By then, he was a hot mess and ready for a nutritious snack. After this near-death experience in an unforgiving triple-canopy jungle – his own Vietnam – Chip was in no mood for light fare. Only a pocket pizza would come close to making up for what he had been through, maybe two…okay three. And it was nutritious because it had cheese in it. Score one for the calcium team!

After every workout, he would delude himself into thinking he had matched effort and skill with elite athletes, ones that got paid for competing in real, physical events. Chip was a master at rationalizing and making big, cognitive leaps.

Chip wiped his brow, sipped his Diet Coke with lime, and spent more than a second debating whether to finish off his second powdered donut before his last meeting for the day.

Chapter 4
A Splash of June

Work wasn't all tight deadlines, overnighters, and sprints to the finish line. Most days, especially this time of the year, were incredibly predictable. Those were the days he could measure by the number of Diet Cokes chugged before the eleven o'clock reports were dumped unceremoniously in his in-box.

Those were the days when Chip felt weak, vulnerable, and judged himself a shadow of what could have been – a hollow shell, existing on dreams and hopes that would never materialize.

Those were the days he would spiral downward until he was under a desk, any desk, curled up and thinking of better days and simpler times.

And then there were days sprinkled between the boring ones when he just liked to have fun with other people's minds.

Chip didn't have much of a mechanical aptitude but, for some reason, had taken to electronics early in life. He understood, intuitively, the basics of wiring, circuits, and switches. He understood how to turn things on and turn things off, which is why he had made his own 'kill switch,' discretely placed under the table and just above his mini-refrigerator.

The switch was connected to the fourth-floor's overhead fluorescent lighting panels so that Chip could control when the lights came on, came off, or when they would flicker. Certain annoying things had to be present for Chip to resort to flickering.

Just knowing he had that kind of power at his fingertips was enough on most days, but on others, it wasn't. Every now, it all just got a little bit too much, and he needed a distraction, a feint, a redirect, and his kill switch did the trick.

Sometimes, someone was near his cubicle for too long; other times, someone was asking him about something or to do something and Chip didn't want to come out and say no but wanted a graceful exit without having to commit or decline on record. Enter the kill switch.

When Chip flipped the switch, the effects were not local – the entire fourth-floor went all dark or flash on and off, depending on Chip's mood.

One moment everything was in balance, everything was right with the world. And then, with a push of a button, the overhead florescent lighting everyone took for granted would flash in two to three-second bursts. This was enough to disrupt any conversation, especially ones involving Chip being asked to do something he didn't want to do.

Chip had gotten out of so many random assignments by flipping the kill switch a few times. No one knew about his secret weapon – the ultimate distractor. No one, except Jimbo, his second-best friend on the floor.

Most days didn't call for the kill switch but ran together just one, big, eternal grind of mind-numbing, accounting work – "Another day at the sausage factory," one of his wittier friends would say.

He wondered where all those years, his hair, the stamp collection, and half his ties had gone. He'd been a spectator rather than a player, although he did like movies and never met a bag of buttered popcorn he didn't like. Make that two.

He would drift into this abyss quite frequently only to be snapped out of its alluring and seductive pull by one thing – the chance to hit the open road, without a map or GPS, on a full tank of gas and feel the wind on his face.

Riding on the open road, feeling the horsepower propel him through time and space reminded him of his obligations to humanity, to his brothers and sisters, to Mother Earth, and to those suffering in Myanmar which he thought was just west of Cincinnati.

After his two-wheeled ride, Chip felt alive and optimistic. He wore bright colors more often. He brushed his teeth and used mouthwash. He leaned forward with all human interactions, especially conversations of any kind. He was refreshed, invigorated, engaged.

The chariot that gave him this freedom and this rush on the open road was by some standards, well, let's just call it for what it is…it was a moped, an all-electric model, the kind you plug in overnight in your garage.

To be clear, Chip did feel the wind on his face when his chariot hit the top speed of thirty-eight miles per hour downhill. It did sound romantic and fearless, but on most workdays, Chip was sensitive to outside temperatures and rising humidity.

Anything below sixty degrees was met bravely but sensibly with a wrap-around balaclava underneath the helmet and a nose clip for good measure (if he didn't feel the pinch something was wrong).

Chip was willing to pay the price for excessive wind on his throat rather than his face.

He refused to listen to music while riding. No pre-loaded playlists and Bluetooth for this maverick. For him, the music got in the way of his connection to nature and the tarmac.

Rather than listen to the kind of music he listened to on his CDs in the Corolla, he preferred no music at all – just the quiet hum of the moped's electric motor. He had gone all-electric years before it had become popular.

He endured insults, a few catcalls, and an occasional roughhousing by the boys in the warehouse, but he knew that one overnight charge saved him pennies every day, and if Chip was nothing else, he was something else when it came to personal finances.

After his usual road trip of six miles (roundtrip), he would shake off self-doubts and arrive to work clearly up for anything. Despite the hoarseness in his throat, he knew he could face the day with confidence.

Others noticed and could tell when he had just come in from one of those trips. Privately, they would say Chip was a different man, more assured. He was called eco-friendly to his face and declared a Virgo in small groups that assembled around the breakroom, a true man for all seasons.

There was no shortage of ride requests around the parking lot from the new hires and the easily influenced. When the sun was out and the possibilities for misadventure endless, Chip considered himself on-call, willing to entertain offers for rides. To his admirers, Chip was a hero who lived life on his own terms.

***

Despite these welcomed episodes of comic relief at other people's expense, daily exercise, and friends to help him through the day, Chip still battled his own demons.

Sometimes, it just got to be too much, and he went to a place where he could shortcut the niceties of human conversation.

He thought about going to such a place last month when people were just becoming too much. So, when he didn't think an online purchase at work would make it through the company firewall, he found, to his delight, he was able to buy a screensaver application that would help manage his frustration with people in more subtle but effective ways.

Chip learned at an early age the power of optical illusions to tap into the subconscious mind. Such knowledge hadn't come cheap. Chip had bought a screensaver app with mystical powers, or at least that is what one of the reviews said.

Thanks to the big online retailers, he was able to get things done at work with less hassle and decidedly more effect through manipulation (strong word but true) of his co-workers involving this new screensaver app.

He bought the app because he knew that technology could advantage him in cutting down the waste built into, of all things, excessive talking at work. *So much time could be saved if he could control more of the conversation,* Chip thought. He might even be doing others a service, he rationalized, by helping them get to their point or, better, Chip's point, faster. Enter the screensaver.

The challenge for Chip was timing.

How long it would take for the 'object' (made it easier to call them that rather than Bill, Jane, or Mike) to be pulled into the dizzying array of moving colors and shapes on his monitor (thank you screensaver app) and become open to Chip's reasonable, work-related requests?

The average time a co-worker took from the moment they were directed to look at Chip's monitor to the time their eyes glazed over and spittle formed on the edge of their mouths was twelve seconds. There had been others with longer lead times.

Each manipulated object (human) had different stress levels or limits – it was quite fascinating.

Jim from Marketing took four seconds.

Alice from corporate had taken a full minute (that had been overly awkward).

Steve, an outsider trying to fit in with a clipboard, hadn't taken the redirects until offered hard candy, wrapped of course.

Usually, one or two 'redirects' would do the trick. Chip wanted to take all the credit, but he understood that the geniuses behind the screensaver application should get all the glory. He wasn't interested in validation, only results.

Chip's requests to his subjects were reasonable and in no way violated their rights…ish. Any individual that approached his cubicle (they were the same thing) with a request that Chip considered too hard, too soon, or just too inconvenient were all subject to the screensaver.

Chip had lost count of how many times his screensaver app had paid for itself. The return on investment was infinity.

The number of requests that had been redirected, turned around, and basically forgotten by the 'subjects' was enough to make most of the days bearable. His only regret was what the screensaver app had done to Paula.

Paula had been just like everyone else. She came to Chip with an 'urgent' request that couldn't wait any longer. It was high priority, she said. Chip was the only one who could help her, and it was due yesterday!

Chip quickly fired up the screensaver with a couple of keystrokes on his keyboard. Paula was asked to look at the monitor quite innocently by Chip.

After six seconds, Paula was glassy-eyed stage, malleable, and ready to be sent away in short order.

Chip, as he had done many times before, told Paula to forget her urgent request, forget who had told her to see Chip, and to forget why she was at Chip's cubicle.

Unfortunately, Chip's finger snap following this instruction had failed to pull Paula out of her trance. Chip went to the next best thing and hit his keyboard key again which disabled the screensaver app.

Paula didn't blink. She didn't want to leave.

She sat there motionless with a nasal drip that wouldn't go away.

It was only after Chip turned up the volume on his radio that belted out some classic '80s that Paula snapped out of her funk.

With dribble running down the side of her mouth, she wistfully mentioned how much she missed going to classic rock concerts where no one cared how you looked or where you were from.

The, in mid-sentence, she turned around and walked across the hallway and into a storage closet that she thought was an elevator.

Chapter 5

Summer in Full Swing

After the manic-induced frenzy of producing the quarterly reports in June, Chip felt justifiably smug about July and decided to ease back the throttle at work, rest on some laurels, and reflect. At his age, he had climbed the corporate ladder about as far as he wanted to go despite the fear of heights.

Sipping on his Diet Coke with lime, he knew he wasn't going to run with the big dogs in corporate-management ranks, but, if one of them offered up pizza to get extra effort from staff, he would do his part –gutting it out and scarfing up extra garlic bread sticks on the way.

As he pondered the possibility of free lunchtime pizza, Chip noticed more of the trivial and frivolous than ever before. There were moments in the day, special moments, where it seemed time was suspended.

Under this power-downed mode, he would see the movement of microscopic dust particles floating through space across the office. He saw connections and connectivity no one else would care to see because they were actually working and didn't have time to look at dust in the air. But Chip had more than enough time most days of the week.

He would watch and observe. Chip would see workers hustling about, talking loudly, emitting their odor, spilling their humanity across the office space. While everyone moved with their energy and their changing mood colors, Chip studied with a content detachment.

From his cubicle, he could see Anthony's coughing, Jill's fake anxiety attacks, the slower-than-usual trash guy, the over-eager junior hires, even the occasional beeping noise from the printer demanding custom paper be manually fed for that oh-so-special print job.

Chip reminisced.

Over his years with the company, he had been there for moments that were etched in history. He mused that if a job ever came up for 'Corporate Storyteller,' he would nominate himself without fuss or fanfare.

There were so many stories to share that had to be begrudgingly told and best delivered through interpretive dancing rather than verbal history or, worse, PowerPoint.

There was the time when the administrative staff nearly walked out *en masse* in 2012 over management's misunderstanding of the difference between an 'assistant' and a 'secretary.'

Words have meaning, and not understanding subtle differences can feed an uprising or stoke a mild uproar.

Chip intervened on principle back then, and, even though his role was never publicly acknowledged, he still received invites to their monthly book club. He walked with a slight limp after that and a greater appreciation for fiction.

Another time, when all the coffee machines on the third floor mysteriously disappeared, Chip wondered if the end was near and his time had come.

There was also an 'almost romance' with Allison from Purchasing who told him more than once that she appreciated the timeliness of his quarterly reports which he thought was code for something else or at least an awkward metaphor.

Chip was thrown off his lofty perch of smugness the last time Allison paid him a compliment by projectile vomiting into a nearby trash can. Chip didn't react well to compliments.

Some came quickly to comfort, but most came to capture the tragedy on video.

He would later thank the gods in heaven that he needed that kind of wake-up call in his middle-aged years before the flirtation went a bit too far. His propensity to blush at the slightest indiscretion kept him at a fairly safe moral distance.

Chip was also married and knew he would never indulge, but flirtation was his way of dancing close to the fire without getting burned.

He didn't have any singe marks, so he had that going for him. Still, sipping on his third soda and reflecting on the present, he felt he was in a relatively good place at this point in his life.

He had work friends, gaming friends, coupon-club friends, etc. There was an inner peace of mind that came from being connected with others that he knew he could count on.

He took a large bite out of a warm donut twist and leaned back on his chair. He had this immediate feeling that his chair was reclining more than usual.

In the time it would normally take for Chip to grab another donut twist from his colleague's cubicle, he realized he was falling backward.

The last thing he saw, as he grasped for anything to reverse his imminent hard landing, was his feet up in the air and his socks visible to the world – they were mismatched, and the color left his face.

This was not the first time this had happened, and it would not be the last. If questioned later by anyone that cared, he would have said that the last coherent thought before the crash of Chip's frame against medium-grade carpet was that too much reflection time has its risks.

As he lay on the floor with so many iPhones around him on record mode, he thought this was the time when his true friends would step in.

Alas, the one helping hand that reached out pried the donut twist from his hand and faded off into the distance. Chip had put up some resistance but given up when he saw the resolve in the eyes of someone much younger and more capable.

Taking away his comfort food when he needed it most was really uncalled for and callous – come on, people!

Not knowing if it was safe to move was when Siena came by his cubicle row to let everyone know the blood-drive van had shown up and all who had signed up should make their way down to the parking lot.

Chip took his time getting up. Everyone had left and had moved on to the next 'shiny object.'

He gingerly made his way down the stairs, holding onto the handrails and feeling quite discombobulated from the fall. His heart started to pick up a little speed.

When he got to the mobile van, it wasn't long before he was strapped down on the stretcher bed with right sleeve rolled up and feeling like a trapped animal. Chip's mind made some quick adjustments.

He drifted into another world, far removed from the constraints of time, space, and gravity. He had to; he and blood drives didn't mix well.

He'd been caught up with the crowd, as usual, and signed up like everyone else when the sign-up roster circulated for the blood drive last month.

It seemed so easy, so appealing when everyone talked about how important it was to give back to the community, etc. But now, here he was, locked down.

He could see others around him, trapped, their pupils dilated. They were scared too. They weren't silently whispering mantras to themselves like Chip was.

Who would bolt first? Chip wondered.

The familiar shakes started, and his mind started to disconnect, leaving him alone for a while. Everyone looked at you when it was your turn to get the blood drawn.

But Chip had checked out. It was only when the concerned nurse invaded his private space that he snapped out of his trance and remembered the last time he was here. Then his next bodily function took over and the cold sweats began.

Chip prided himself on showing strength when needed and reminded himself that others were watching, like self-coaching had ever worked before.

The junior staff on the fourth-floor, those he thought counted on him for so many things, were a motley crew of early to mid-twenty somethings who he'd grown fond of over the past year or two. They would be counting on him to be an example of what it means to be a good corporate citizen on this blood drive.

If he could get through this without others noticing, he would be able to shine for those he mentored and loved. But when Chip felt that first prick of the needle, he would later recount what could only be described as an out-of-body experience.

He never looked at the needle, but he didn't have to. The nurse gave it away with the classic line, "…now you should just feel a pinch." At that point, Chip tensed up his whispered mantras which were now audible to the nurse who tried to move quickly.

When it happened, it happened fast. Without the slightest embarrassment, Chip let out a muted yelp that was as guttural as it was feminine. He didn't care.

In his mind, he was in mortal danger. Fight or flee, definitely flee. His mini howl would have been embarrassing enough if he hadn't followed it up with a plea to the nurse to stop what she was doing and move onto the next person.

This was not the nurse's first rodeo, so she kept smiling and kept going. She needed the blood.

Watching Chip squirm, curse, and gyrate was like watching a train wreck. The others simply couldn't look away. This was not the calm, assured, and nerdy Chip who had interviewed each of them for their first job after college graduation.

The smile could only last so long. The nurse called for help immediately and an on-the-spot consult. Someone swapped out a bag and Chip was sedated without permission.

Apparently, the American Red Cross has the discretion to go from nice, homely blood-donation service to emergency-room conditions if required, and Chip required it, without a doubt.

His nurse couldn't recall the last time something like this had happened, maybe during her first year and she was easily pushing seventy. Her smile usually worked.

Chip was carried out of the blood-drive van on a stretcher, strapped to his new best friend – the oxygen tank. There was some incoherent babbling, but then again, babbling usually was incoherent. Not to Chip though.

In his mind, he was relaying instructions to the stretcher-bearer to take care of his 1:00 p.m. meeting, oblivious to the fact that the stretcher-bearer was not a fellow accountant on the fourth-floor. And stretcher-bearers thought all meetings were optional, so what was the big deal about any meeting?

For the next few hours at the local hospital, Chip was put officially under observation but unofficially consigned to his new normal, slowly coming out of his induced stupor and reflecting that were easier ways to end his voluntary participation in the blood drive.

There was some comfort that he knew things would/could/should only get better. He would feel the metaphorical sun on his back again and the wind on his face.

***

Chip had a recurring eye twitch, mostly from nerves, but he wasn't discounting that it could be hereditary. He never talked about it with anyone except his inanimate friend, Bill. He was able to control it most of the time, but it was temperamental and sometimes moody if it didn't get what it wanted, which was airtime, a chance to show off in front of others.

He did what he could, but there were times when he wasn't sure who was in charge – his mind or those contrarian eyelids of his.

Chip wanted compensation, maybe an allowance, for his 'disability,' so he didn't think it was much of a leap to try to get a permanent parking-permit pass signed off by a local doctor that would have sympathy for him and his eye twitch.

What was the worst that could happen? Chip asked himself. Sure, maybe outright rejection and some wounded pride, but Chip had always wanted that coveted blue handicapped pass and loved the portability of it all. So he went for it.

Making the case that an eye-twitch condition was reasonable grounds for parking privileges was not as difficult as you might think. Chip and Doctor 'Bob,' another one of his college roommates that had joined the medical ranks and stayed local, was the first person he thought of to attempt this *coup de grace*.

Convincing Doctor Bob to sign off on the application for Chip was the easy part. It was really just a quick conversation and five minutes of paperwork. That was the easy part. Convincing his colleagues that he was deserving of such a privilege was a different matter entirely.

He shouldn't have surprised him on how quickly he was questioned about his new parking spot, the one that required a handicapped parking permit.

They saw him park in the blue spot from their shaded windows. Chip was now an object of curiosity/ scorn/jealousy.

Five minutes ago, he was one of them – now, he was different and must be confronted or at least questioned. Some things didn't make sense on the fourth-floor, and those parking spots were always empty.

One of his colleagues mounted the most credible line of inquiry about Chip's new blue passport and her name was Dianne, spelled with two 'n's' and a silent 'e.'

Dianne didn't like Chip, never had, but still purported to be his friend. Chip was clueless about Dianne, her intentions, and her ambition to knock Chip off his popularity perch on the floor. She wanted to be the one that others came to for advice and mentoring. It was time for the gloves to come off.

"Hi, Chip – I didn't know you had a disability."

There was a brief pause, then she continued, "Some wounds are invisible to the eye, I guess?" It was definitely much more of a question than a statement.

Dianne had made sure that there was at least one or two of Chip's other friends with her when she met him at his cubicle. Coups rarely happen in the quiet of the day and away from a crowd.

"What exactly is your disability?" she tried to say it innocently like she honestly cared, but it didn't come across that way. Dianne didn't wait for an answer.

"My dad had a handicapped parking permit – but he lost both legs in Vietnam. He was a war hero – walked through a rice paddy to try and save his buddies."

Dianne looked around. Heads popped up over the partition walls and some left their cubicles and started to move slowly toward Chip's cubicle where Dianne was just getting started. Dianne wanted all of this.

This was her moment, and she needed a crowd.

Chip's other friends were a little confused about what was going on. Dianne wasn't confused. She was a cold, calculating accountant who could turn it on and off as needed to get what she wanted. And, right now, Dianne wanted to take over the pack, Chip's pack.

"The only joy he felt from his service in his later years was when he was dying from Agent Orange exposure. And the only thing that gave him pleasure in his later years was guaranteed parking at his favorite grocery store."

Oh, she was good, Chip thought. He also thought the best attacks always come from the flanks and not the front. Dianne was flanking him.

She knew she had proverbially pinned Chip to the wall with that latest vignette about her dad who, by the way, had never served a day of life in uniform. He was a retired rural postal worker that loved his kids, the Steelers, and his renovated basement.

Sure, he loved the military like most others, but he couldn't tell you where Vietnam was or half of the states in the union. Still, to Dianne, her dad was a convenient pawn in her chess game with Chip.

She had Chip right where she wanted. Chip knew he had to answer. But what to say? Doctor 'Bob' signed the authorization with a nudge and a wink. He couldn't let that one out. Chip hadn't the time to prepare a cover. So, he jumped right in – both feet first.

Shifting eyes, a little shuffle on the feet followed by a fake but believable long sigh, then…

"It's a little hard to talk about, Dianne, but something traumatic happened at an early age and I've developed a chronic nervous condition manifested through right eye twitches that happen when I am under stress."

He liked the combination of manifested and stress because, together, they sounded clinical and had a certain medical authenticity about it.

Believable? he asked himself. Perhaps, he thought, but he knew this would not end today. The first moves had happened. Dianne had the edge because she had the advantage of surprise.

She wouldn't have such an advantage moving forward. Chip would be ready.

The die was cast – the chess pieces were in place. *How easily we can misjudge someone,* Chip thought.

For the next couple of weeks, Dianne spent most of her free time watching Chip, usually through carefully placed mirrors.

She watched him in staff meetings, other staff meetings she wasn't part of, walking down the hallways, interacting with his cubicle officemates, even observed his trips to the soda machine. She would follow him to the cafeteria; he was easy to follow – so predictable.

She was obsessed; she kept a journal.

Chip knew he was under the microscope, him and his blue parking permit, so he was careful, very careful.

When someone would ask for Chip to do something that the slightest bit inconvenient, Chip would twitch his right eye, showing the world that such things created undue stress on Chip.

He knew he was being watched and couldn't let his guard down, so he had to remember to keep his right eye twitching, especially when people walked by.

He wouldn't make a big deal of it – just look at the person, wince slightly, and let the right eyelid do its thing in a controlled ten-second burst.

Most people understood that they'd crossed the line and triggered something that could have been avoided. Some stayed for a second ten-second burst because they were a little slow on the uptake.

Through all of this, Dianne watched and waited.

She would stay in pursuit of her goal to expose and to defraud. Her next move, though, would be her last.

On a mundane Wednesday, just seven days after her confrontation with Chip, she hid in a supply closet and waited for her moment.

If Chip got eye twitches when nervous or scared, then, in theory, he should go into twitch mode in his right eye when she would jump out of the closet and scare him, as a practical joke of course.

Her plan was simple. Catch Chip not twitching when he should have.

It didn't work out the way she wanted.

When it happened, Chip's eye went into simulated twitch mode, just like he had practiced.

His scouts had alerted him beforehand that she was hiding in the supply closet.

He had paid them a little extra to keep watch, and, knowing the rhythm and pace of the workweek, he counted on something like this from her on a Wednesday rather than any other day of the week.

In Chip's world, when you challenge Chip, you better go big or go home, and going home meant literally going home or at least leaving the fourth-floor, never to return, especially when someone practices disability discrimination, if that was a thing, and Chip was fairly sure that was a thing.

Dianne's prank got all the press Chip had hoped for. Management was brought in.

There were 'listening sessions' in small groups about the importance of respecting other people's disabilities. Dianne had gone too far and something had to be done.

Within two weeks, Dianne was quietly relocated to the San Diego office – no moving allowance, and a smaller cubicle.

***

Dianne was gone and his blue handicapped parking permit was safe. This was cause for celebration. He would venture out more, explore more of the building, really explore the whole corporate space. Maybe it was time to go to the basement and see some folks he hadn't seen in a while. The type of people he wanted to see after the stress of nearly being outed was a special type, the type who you visited and not the other way round.

When Chip wanted to engage with a class of people the polar opposite of his accounting colleagues, he would hit the 'B' button on the elevator and take a trip to the wild side. The basement had only one functioning work area – the mailroom where you weren't judged, and the corduroy was always in style. A trip to the mailroom was always a trip into the unknown.

Picking up the mail was the last thing on Chip's mind as he descended below ground in the maintenance elevator to the one destination that could enrich his life...at least for this Thursday. When he stepped into that room, he was in another time, another place, confronted with new images, sounds, and smells.

In the mailroom, Chip felt alive and it scared him a little. A dizzying array of characters – some of them human – met him at the door with their honesty, smiles, and trinkets. If he was honest with himself, which he tried not to be, there was a little bit more of the mailroom in Chip than he liked to admit.

In the basement, more than any other place, Chip felt like a modern-day Ernest Hemingway – part of the true working class from a bygone era – a man in the moment, in the trenches, but with an eye out for possible paper cuts in the most obvious of places. There were never accountants in the basement; math didn't work down there.

Chip's first stop was the poker game in one of the dark corners of the mailroom that seemed to have no end and no beginning. Chip breathed in the heavy cigar smoke but refused a drink. He never accepted a drink from anyone in the mailroom – he just couldn't be sure what was in it.

There was always a poker game happening. The fire alarms had been disabled for just such occasions. He didn't know how to play, what the rules were, or even why money and digital watches were flung in the center of the table. But that didn't matter.

The looks on the players told him all he needed to know about the difference between locals in the mailroom and everyone else that dragged through life 'upstairs.'

It was up there, in places like the fourth-floor especially, where convention, rules, and protocols kept people at arm's reach from each other, or so they thought.

Here in the mailroom, he was safe from those that lived privileged lives and forced their idiosyncrasies and petty rules on others.

In the mailroom, more than any place else, he was safe from the stares of the beautiful people. These were the ones that set the rules on the floors above. They were the elites who needed no formal titles to get things done, only pedigree and all the right connections.

They came in many shapes and sizes, many colors. They were above the fray; they were the beautiful people.

They were few in numbers but easy to spot, impossible to become. When they approached you, you did the double blink, dropped the eyes, and (if there was time) a curtsy of some sort (nobody laughed when you did it).

They didn't walk, they floated.

Their posture was incorruptible.

Their traded currency was relationships and power, not cash or credit.

They didn't speak, they imparted.

They didn't listen, they tolerated.

They always had a full head of hair – natural, no surgeries.

You either were or you were not.

They ran the place, any place.

They were not management – they had their own shadow government, their own leadership chain.

Chip knew his place and there was comfort in that; there was predictability, consistency. Most, like Chip, intuitively knew not to initiate, only to respond.

Sitting next to the poker players, Chip thought long and hard about the difference between life upstairs and downstairs, especially when it came to the beautiful people.

Down here in the grit, the grime, and the smoke, Chip felt detached from his life upstairs and that made him feel like he had hit the pause button for just a while. He was safe from beautiful people while he was down there in the mailroom where the mail came in but where most of it stayed.

Beautiful people perplexed him. He wasn't jealous of them; he just couldn't neatly bin them into a category or put them in a box. They weren't manipulable.

There were three occasions in the past four years when Chip had conversed with one of them; two of the occasions had been a misdial on his phone which had been promptly handled by someone else.

Both times, he recognized the voice on the line and knew he was being recorded. Despite a rising body temperature and sudden onset of tunnel vision, he pulled through and everything returned to normal.

Each interaction was something to savor, to treasure, to imprint in the permanent memory bank, and Chip's memory bank was far from full.

They went by other names, less appealing ones like 'alphas,' 'meat-eaters,' etc. But, to Chip, they were the ones to watch and carefully so.

He didn't mind that they would complete his sentences or even pick at his food. It didn't matter. Their time was precious, and they only had so much time to give before floating out of the room and onto the next event.

They were the ones that could get by with three hours of sleep a day or run a six-minute mile pace (uphill and backward) before a breakfast which was always continental and always plant-based.

They wore a slight smile as if it to say, "I'm listening, but think really, really carefully about what to say to me – take your time, this is important…but abbreviate in bullet points for your sake and mine."

When it was clear someone was not getting to the point fast enough, they threw convention to the wind and motioned them to hurry in exaggerated but controlled facial and hand expressions.

They were always on-message, never lost, and never carried cash.

They never committed to anything or anyone unless it was to each other.

They never wrote emails (can be traced) and always explained important things on whiteboards which were quickly erased by their assistants.

Their footprints were faint and vanishing – all things were temporary.

To be in the company of a beautiful person was to be suspended in time, temporarily free of worldly concerns and gravity. In their presence, you were either being schooled, edified, or both.

Their techniques were well-known. Intimidation, then submission, then intimidation again, just for good measure.

In what seemed like a past life, Chip remembered his encounter with Janice from Sales. It started out innocently when Janice called Chip by another name in the hallway on the fourth-floor.

"Hi, Jethro," she said casually and kept walking and didn't look back.

Jethro? Chip thought. He was confused again. *My name isn't Jethro*, he thought.

She said it as if Chip had always been Jethro and known by no other name. Chip reacted with a puzzled look but continued to walk down the hallway – *it's nice to be noticed even if she gets my name wrong*, he thought.

Chip considered those in Sales to be, without exception, made up of mostly the beautiful people, so someone like Janice probably knew something he didn't.

Maybe his name really was Jethro, and someone had played a cruel joke on him since birth. Stranger things have happened, he reasoned, as he had made his way safely to the breakroom.

Chip didn't know anyone called Jethro, but his mind went into overdrive about what a Jethro might look like.

This took him on a breathtaking ride to strange and magical places he was not expecting to see. Jethro! Where did they get that name from?

When Chip thought of someone called Jethro, he thought of sorcery, mystique, dungeons, dragons, clerics, flowing dreadlocks, maybe some '80s hair band music.

He particularly liked flowing dreadlocks imagery on account of his receding hairline that had abruptly shown up in his early thirties and never left.

Chip had good reason to be suspicious and a little anxious when he was invited up to the fifth floor later that day by Janice who saw him along the same hallway.

She was wearing a different outfit and might have had a haircut or a new hairstyle. Something was different. He wasn't.

Chip followed Janice into the elevator. She said nothing and Chip, being an accountant, certainly would not initiate conversation.

As they exited the elevator, they both made their way into an office marked 'Sales Conference Room.' Chip noticed that the entire fifth floor seemed unnaturally quiet, even for sales.

Janice opened the door to the conference room and walked in. He followed only to be greeted by sales staff who burst into a Happy Birthday song for…Jethro.

Some other non-beautiful people had decorated the room for the occasion, but they weren't invited to stay. The beautiful people had calendared this event for a special purpose and that purpose was Chip.

They kept singing. Chip didn't know there were multiple verses to the birthday song, but they did. In the second verse, one of them brought out the large foam birthday hat and put it on Chip's head with a smirk.

They say the eyes are the gateway to the soul, but Chip's eyes were obscured from view due to the large foam birthday hat they stuffed over his head, his nose, and down to his mouth which was slightly open.

Not able to see the crowd any longer, thanks to the hat, Chip chose acceptance over resistance. He would answer to Jethro. If this is what it took to gain their trust, then he was all in. He was Jethro – a man of the moment, unrestrained by rules and convention.

He was an adopted son of the sales team. This was the ticket to fifth-floor access and privileges, and he would ride this train until asked to leave.

July and August blurred together as Chip reflected on his alternate name which was growing on him.

Chip prided himself on getting through the summer relatively intact but thought long and hard about where the fall might take him. In the days, weeks, and months ahead, there would be people to avoid, assignments to dodge, reports to delay, and deadlines to shift without attribution.

Such was Chip's lot in life, and it was all manageable as long as the curve balls weren't too curvy, and the surprises weren't too surprisey.

Chapter 6

The Leaves Are Falling

Chip Was Hungry.

It was late September and the month was nearly over without Chip losing any bets, giving away anything of value, or getting pulled into dodgy side deals that cost more than they should.

It was also a Wednesday, and if there was ever a time to forget to pack his lunch, it was Wednesdays. There had been no forgetting, quite the opposite.

Mrs. Clementine insisted he make his own lunch during the work. But, each Wednesday, Chip would routinely call his wife back, saying he had forgotten to make his lunch and not to worry, he would figure something out.

Mrs. Clementine suffered through this weekly charade knowing that Chip missing a meal or two might not be such a bad thing. He could lose a few.

But what she didn't know was that being a Wednesday, Chip was going to be just fine, more than fine, in taking care of his gastronomical needs. Wednesdays were potluck days.

Throughout the corporate building, in almost every department, on Wednesdays, some team somewhere hosted an office potluck, a get-together of donated hot dishes cooked at home and brought in to share with colleagues.

He didn't understand why potlucks weren't on Fridays, but he had given up on that logic a long time ago. The best he could come up with was that there was a human need to celebrate 'hump day,' the middle day of week, and celebrating the arrival of such a day with food meant that, chronically speaking, there were fewer days left to get to the weekend than before. Thus, the potlucks.

On every workday lunchtime period, Chip stayed in his cubicle and ate quietly like a mouse. On Wednesdays, he was a warrior, a hunter. Chip would be on the hunt for free food.

Some of the reasons were many for such an event – celebrate a birthday, build team spirit, lift office morale after a tough project, etc. Chip didn't care what the reason was – he was hungry. Chip was not going to skip a meal. Quite the opposite. Today, he might eat the equivalent of two or three.

This was not his first rodeo. Timing was everything or nothing – there was no middle ground when it came to potlucks.

It was 11:15 a.m. and he would beat the rush to most of the prime potlucks if he moved quickly and with purpose.

He kept note on his competition and noticed that they started out their rounds at 11:45 – idiots! This strategy defined them, in Chip's mind, as scavengers more than hunters, willing to accept scraps others left behind at makeshift dining tables.

The second floor was his first go-to floor, home to the Purchasing Division who tended to go for Italian-themed spreads.

Their garlic bread was baked on-premises and their meatballs cooked all morning, sending wafts of garlic up and down the building. They were proud of their heritage and flaunted it through food. Good for them! Bravo Italia!

They never asked who he was because Chip smiled a lot and carried a clipboard. Clipboards answered a lot of questions.

Chip could easily smell lasagna in the air when he started out on his planned route and followed his nose.

The third floor had an awkward layout, so he had to really pay attention to get where he needed to go with minimal double backs and re-routes.

The signs were obvious to the trained eye (and nose) – an empty cubicle cleared for one reason only: crockpots covered and plugged in on 'warm' setting, cardboard plates still in plastic wrap, and nervous faces wondering when someone with authority would signal for everyone to begin the feast.

Chip was in his element. The meatballs were amazing, the garlic bread divine. The sparkling apple juice was also a nice touch.

With most of the potlucks he deliberately stumbled upon, he found that he could remain anonymous and not have to introduce himself or explain why he was there to eat their food and then leave as quickly as he came. *I love this country*, he mused.

Most people didn't question who he was or if he had 'contributed' to the menu, mainly because he smiled a lot and spoke even less. He just blended in and looked like the type of person that worked with them but was squirreled away most of the time in some back area, alone and left out by the rest of them.

Maybe, when they looked at Chip, they felt guilty that they had not approached him sooner. So, at some of these potlucks, Chip got offered more food than he could handle by over-caring (but guilty) 'co-workers' that felt food could solve their lack of manners.

But not everyone was like the Purchasing Department. He'd only been confronted once and aggressively at that, but Chip found other ways to get even with the individual without compromising other potluck routes.

He looked at his digital watch. 1150 hrs. He went with the twenty-four-hour format because it made him connected with more manly professions, like soldiering or park rangering.

Twenty-four-hour time settings somehow made him feel that his workday had to be accounted for in very discrete minutes and seconds like he was on a series of military missions requiring a start and a stop.

Chip was totally stuffed – barely able to move. The hyenas (i.e., those that started out on a potluck scavenger hunt much later than Chip) showed up, but most were questioned by a friendly but firm face or two before being politely turned away.

Chip smirked as they skulked off. They never learned. had chalked up another successful potluck run. He went back to his cubicle and carved a small notch on the side of his desk to record the event for posterity. Every free lunch was a notch for inner bragging rights.

To feed his competitive drive, if you could call it that, he never settled for anything less than two successful potluck visits during lunch.

The Italian food had been a great starter, but he had finished his second potluck run on the first floor with Human Resources who had some crazy, South Asian dishes that had a done a number on him.

***

Back in his cubicle, the last thing he wanted to do was prepare the weekly report for management. As he checked his Facebook page one last time, the phone rang and a number popped up he didn't recognize, since he saved the phone number in his directory each time he got a call even if it was in error.

Chip doubted any call into his cubicle was an error and tagged each one of those to his latest conspiracy theory of how the world works and doesn't.

In this particular call, the young lady on the line was polite and professional which made Chip suspect immediately. It was the doctor's office. The doctor wanted to see him right away about the results of the biopsy they had taken a couple of weeks ago.

"What were the results?" he asked over the phone.

"The doctor would prefer to meet you in person. Can you meet first thing Monday morning, October 1st?"

"Uhm, sure," he replied.

He put the phone down and stared at his monitor and then his ears started to twitch. He'd not been this nervous since Jonathan, his last boss, had quit a year ago with only two days' notice. Not everyone can hack it in accounting, Chip thought at the time. But then Susan, a senior manager, from the third floor had stopped by and asked Chip to fill in for Jonathan until they got a proper manager in.

She needed Chip to take the lead on a 'hot' process improvement project that was floundering.

"This is just temporary," Susan assured Chip. "And, of course, you get the manager's parking spot." Chip could see the desperation in her face.

He didn't know that Susan had tried to pin this tail on other donkeys with different bribes and inducements. No one wanted to touch this project, no one. So, she had moved on to Chip, her absolute lowest-ranked candidate.

Susan was desperate. Her next raise was probably rising on the success or failure of this initiative, and all initiatives need a project manager. She continued.

After no response from Chip, she said what Chip would have predicted coming from any corporate talking head, "You can do this!" she said to Chip in an attempt to be motherly.

It sorts of worked. Chip raised his eyebrows and made eye contact. Susan was encouraged.

"Everyone does their turn in the barrel, Chip."

She said 'barrel' as if she knew that place all too well. It still sounded forced though. Her eyes didn't match her facial expressions, her mouth, her words. Everything was off.

They stared at each other a little longer than was appropriate for the situation. Then, she finally spoke in an even quieter voice in case someone overheard them.

"I'll give you a small expense account to handle off-hour expenses at your discretion," her voice was a whisper, more of a plea. And she said it as if both had known all along there was more in Susan's tank to give. He knew tactical patience had paid off.

He said yes, in equally hushed tones, and they agreed to meet in the morning. Chip knew that she was unsure about whether this would work. Chip and Susan had a history – three weeks of history, and he still hadn't figured out what happened – so fast, so confusing.

He hadn't broken any vows or anything, just maybe had gotten a bit too comfortable in each other's presence. He took the job on one more condition which was confirmed the following morning.

"Susan," his confidence had roared back now that yesterday was behind him and she had brought him a fresh coffee and a blueberry muffin.

"I want full access to the corporate gym." He'd never completed an actual workout in his life, but she already knew that. It was how it sounded that mattered to Chip, not Susan.

"I want the email system updated to reflect my new title and a bigger expense budget to cover what I need to win over key staff on this project."

That last request was pushing it a bit – that translated to at least two lunches out each week with one of his buddies from procurement and another in the basement who no one knew what he did; he just smiled a lot.

She said yes quickly; too quickly, she would recall later. And so, the deal was struck again (no physical touch – just a nod) and Chip was a manager.

It lasted one day.

Chip never worked on a 'process improvement' project but knew, from a podcast, that a successfully led project 'on his watch' was likely a clear signal to leadership that he was ready for this and more.

His first and last day, although he didn't know it at the time, began early with two, maybe three donuts and some whole milk. After a quick scan of the subject lines of his emails, he decided to delete them all and start with a clean inbox.

He had done something like that before but with someone else's inbox. This was an all-new experience and he kind of liked it.

He then had his assistant send out a calendar invite for his first team meeting, after lunch of course. He was eager to get runs on the board, so a team meeting was a good place to start. He knew this was going to be hard work, but he knew that the smarter people in the room (everyone else if he was honest) would help him navigate the nuances of whatever process they had to improve. It takes a village!

That afternoon, the party faithful filed into the conference room for Chip's first team meeting. Shannon, the new assistant, made sure the whiteboards were clean and inviting.

Chip had to get this right. He'd watched managers before, how they spoke (clipped), acted, breathed (shallow), and even dressed. He was ready, except for the dressed part.

He had the room set the best way he thought would encourage brainstorming, innovation, and creativity. Lighting, post-it notes at the ready, and bowls of mid-tier chocolate in bowls strategically placed around one of the tables. He was ready.

Chip walked to the middle of the room and waited. When the fifteen individuals arrived on time and way too eager, he was brief and to the point.

"Ladies and gentlemen and Jim." Jim was one of his buddies that always laughed when he did that.

"I am honored to head up this important initiative for the company. We have three days to map out the current process, identify problems, and recommend solutions."

Chip looked down at his clipboard to make sure he was still on message. He was.

"I am putting Dave in charge of the first part, Hannah in charge of the second part, and my colleague (really Chip's best friend who just wanted a diversion that afternoon), Billy Joe Jim Bob (aka Jim), in charge of the third part. What are your questions?"

The worker bees were confused. They needed more, much more. Clarification. Explanation. Context.

Chip's new assistant, Allison, thought immediately they needed a new manager. But she was getting paid to advise on management selections, at least not yet.

Chip chose to ignore the rising volume of questions. He continued.

"On the table in front of me, you'll find crayons of all different types of colors, butcher block paper, some chewing gum, three water bottles, and the key to this conference room." Now for the fun part.

"When I leave, you'll be locked in this room." Chip paused for effect as if pausing let everyone know who was in charge.

"I've also provided baby wipes for hygiene purposes," he said matter-of-factly.

"I'll check in tomorrow and get an update from your team leads. I know you'll do great things."

He was just about to leave. Hands shot up instantly.

Chip ignored them until the hands went down one by one. He walked confidently out of the room and locked the door behind him. Someone started laughing. Another tried to leave, but the tables were blocking their exit path. Allison barely made it out in time.

Since the team leads were clueless and the worker bees were perplexed, as they were now in a locked room, everyone looked at each other and then to the door.

For historical purposes, it should be carefully noted and chronicled that Chip's foray into management from his first public address until the time he was officially fired/released from all management duties and sent back to his cubicle was one hour and twenty-three minutes. Here was the rundown.

The first hour was a sight to see in that large conference room. Fifteen alpha males and alpha females locked in a room, egging each other on, fighting for control, and eager to exploit any sign of weakness in each other.

At the top of the hour, someone or something broke and the next few minutes were spent by the first team leader and his crew trying to break through the door while the others looked on sheepishly.

The door wouldn't open.

Chip was watching this on the other side of the door and wondering why they weren't using the crayons to color and draw things like process maps or organizational charts.

Through the glass, Chip could make out some of the words they were mouthing at him but not all.

Chip remained stoic, calm even. He knew this was team storming at its finest and all teams have to get through this before they can progress to a higher form of interdependency and team effectiveness.

Again, another podcast informing Chip how to be a manager.

One brave soul from Purchasing opened a window in an attempt to escape the locked conference room. She made it out on the ledge but slipped and fell twenty feet into bushes that were the pretty but prickly type.

Her screams were heard by the first-floor staff and help readily came up the stairs to the room only to find it locked. When pressed, Chip produced the key and asked Allison to unlock the door.

People ran in all directions, back to their offices, but some left the building. And some never came back, not the next day, not ever.

In fact, some would say they just kept running and never looked back at their fourth-floor jobs and their fourth-floor cubicles and their fourth-floor breakroom.

For many, this was their first team project in the company, and for the younger ones, it was their first team period. They would be forever warped based on what they saw and heard that day, hardened individualists resisting all forms of teamwork, thanks to Chip's little experiment.

This would take time to process on many levels. Some, if they were honest with themselves, were not sure they could look the others in the eyes and say they had conducted themselves professionally.

Things had been said in the heat of the moment that, well, were best expressed in the mind rather than out loud.

Susan did not have much time to put this genie back in the bottle and called an 'all hands' meeting over the intercom.

But it was too late. The process-improvement team members of the shortest-lived process-improvement team in history were scattered to the four winds.

The emergency meeting would have to wait until tomorrow. Susan, with her strained voice over the intercom, tried and failed to assure others that mental health professionals would be available, on-site.

Chip wasn't aware of those recent developments with his team until the email, from Susan, flashed across his monitor that the team had been disbanded due to operational reasons and safety concerns.

Susan acted swiftly, realizing that the longer she delayed decisive action, the harder it would be to shake off this debacle. Chip was ushered into Susan's office where her boss, Peter, was standing to the side, arms crossed, wearing a slight grin.

Peter's rise to management had been less conventional than Susan's, punctuated by projects, like Chips, but managed to completion.

Peter understood Chip and his potential but gave a reluctant nod to Susan's handling of the situation. Plus, human resources were in the room and he couldn't act anything less than displeased in front of those that represented all things appropriate and politically correct at the company.

In sum, Chip was given two weeks' paid vacation, effective immediately, and signed a form that he didn't get a chance to read.

Chip had certainly misread the gravity of the situation. He considered his approach to office meetings revolutionary, not successful this time, but others would meet with success following his playbook, he reasoned.

Chip knew he'd set a new standard.

With the right people, some crayons, a locked conference room, and no bathroom breaks, he could get results!

Part 2
October Surprise

Chapter 7

Doctor 'Raj'

Monday, October 1st, was fast approaching and, with it, his appointment with Doctor Raj, an old school friend who lived and practiced locally. Chip's anxiety level steadily climbed as the day got closer. *If his biopsy results were negative, they would have just called me*, he thought.

Chip wasn't used to being completely in control and it was unfamiliar territory for him. He lived his life by scheduling, and scheduling meant he was in control, not someone or something else.

His well-used planner was a work of art and beauty – everything was written in fine-point pencil with events, meetings, and appointments neatly recorded, rarely erased. That planner was an extension of his personality, a mirror into his soul.

In the back and front of this planner were his goals broken down by category, careful to keep his professional and personal lives separate.

He lived his life, hour to hour, day to day, and week to week, and maybe the first few months – all neatly chronicled, planned, and thought through.

There was no room or space in his planner for anything that he had not planned for or thought about…ever. Until now.

By his reckoning, being asked to come in for an appointment could mean only one thing about his biopsy – bad news and thinking about bad news meant bad sleep.

When Chip didn't sleep well, he defaulted quickly to binge-watching, and nothing said binge-watching like a mini-series about a post-apocalyptic world without electricity and enough subplots to feed an appetite for onion-flavored, sourdough pretzels. Chip was like that.

When daylight arrived on a drizzly, cold Saturday morning, Chip was halfway through season two of a B-grade zombie series.

The next episode was as predictable as the last, so he took a break, restocked on the pretzels, and decided to make a plan for the rest of his day. It wasn't even 7 a.m. yet and Chip felt an urgency to complete his plan for the day. He was antsy.

Chip loved to make plans and lists, but mostly lists and always in pencil. He knew enough about himself to know that he was quick to judge and harshly at that.

If he saw someone using pen, rather than pencil, to write in their calendars, they were mentally binned in a category of people who shouldn't drive or check out books from the library.

Chip planned his time in fifteen-minute increments, even on weekends – especially on weekends. He was fearful of unstructured time and thought unplanned anything was a mark of shame. So, he kept busy doing something even if that something was not really anything at all other than helping him pass the time.

Surprisingly, he hadn't woken Mrs. Clementine since waking up abruptly in the middle of the night. She was usually a very light sleeper. While she slept on, a text message flashed across his smartphone.

He was grateful for the distraction since he'd run out of ideas for how to fill up most of his afternoon. The morning was fine, but the afternoon was a blank canvas. People like Chip didn't like blank canvasses.

The text was from a colleague, one from a very short list of people who Chip socialized with afterhours. It was an invitation for Saturday night karaoke at his local bar/pub.

Ahhh, karaoke. He was always up for karaoke with friends, and given what may or may not happen next at the doctor's office, his ego needed a lift. Suddenly, his Saturday evening was booked, penciled in, and boxed out. Boom!

Karaoke was just the thing he needed right now. He needed a distraction or maybe several. But invitations for karaoke were met with mixed emotions.

There was no doubt in his mind he had talent, the kind that stops people in mid-sentence or holds up traffic. Chip knew when it came to his vocal cords, he could be a little over the top, but, he reasoned, it's not bragging if you can back it up. And Chip, in his mind, could back it up.

He was called by a higher power to share his talent with others, and the karaoke bar was his second home, or, at least, that's how Chip saw things. That is where he could dazzle, entertain, and poach some free spinach dip for services rendered, free of charge.

On the other hand, he never understood why everyone didn't appreciate his turn on the mike. Chip tolerated the catcalls, the jeers, even the hissing. He knew that others wanted something they didn't have themselves – a voice that comes once in a generation. That would be his voice.

Chip wasn't one for the spotlight, or so he told himself. From a young age, he was told he had a gift, by his favorite, senile grandmother, and it was his to share with the world. He was special, she told him.

His grandmother never actually said what his gift was; she never got to that part. Chip assumed it was his voice and just went with it.

There weren't too many places to share one's singing talents with others. Sure, there were family get-togethers and the odd, impromptu solo gig at someone's wedding or bar-mitzvah.

But the karaoke bar was a guaranteed performance whenever he showed up. They made a space for him always and without fail.

Chip's singing had a way of getting the audience off the chairs and on their feet, some might say jazzed up. Chip would say jazzed. In truth, others, not emotionally invested, would say irritated and amped up.

But ignorance is bliss, and, for now, Chip's place to shine, to release, to entertain was his local karaoke bar, an Irish pub most days of the week except Saturdays when the projector screen was wheeled from the back and placed prominently by the bar.

It was subtle but effective. If you wanted to sing a number, you should buy a drink while you're at it.

Chip took for granted there were those in the crowd who weren't as passionate about his choice of songs or maybe jealous of his vocal range.

He knew most of the crowd were astute enough to know when they were about to be inspired, and the inspired part was when Chip would walk on the stage and share what he had with this part of the world.

He saw singing at the karaoke bar as more philanthropic than anything else. He was giving without any expectation of receiving. He would not accept fame or fortune for what he wanted to give freely to those in his community. He was giving for giving's sake.

But Chip still experienced some shakes, some might say a little stage fright, as the night progressed and the '80s songs seemed to get louder and louder in the Irish pub.

He knew his turn was coming but would have to wait for the right moment. The right moment always came because someone preceding him would usually suck at singing and he felt obligated to make it right somehow with the crowd who deserved more.

Chip's underlying concern whenever he performed was not performance anxiety in the usual sense but more a fear of being spotted by a talent scout who wanted to take him places he didn't want to go…yet.

Chip was a part-time artiste – his true love would always be accounting, not show business. He didn't want to go global with his voice – keeping it local and doing it for free was his mantra, his code.

He did what he did for his friends and anybody else that happened to be there. Chip knew all his life that he could sing, sing well enough to be paid in food, maybe cash. But that wasn't the point.

If asked, and sometimes he wished he was asked more often, whether his vocal range was more associated with one genre or another, he would shrug and say he gave the audience what they needed, not wanted.

Talent cut across genres and Chip never made too much adjustment to the size, shape, or demographics of the crowd. They would figure it out, he mused.

He would take any request, as long as it was in English and was not anything from The Eurythmics. Their lyrics cut too deep. He couldn't go there – too painful.

It wasn't unfair to say he struggled with his gift. He knew he had a responsibility to the world. He would ask himself constantly whether on that night or any other karaoke night if 'they' were ready, ready for him.

It was this burning question on Chip's mind each time he walked up on the stage.

The crowd's reactions were never a surprise. Facial expressions confirmed worst fears whenever he let loose – he was a freak of nature, a prodigy, a singing sensation.

Looking at the crowd with their rants and mindless screams said it all, or at least said what Chip thought they were saying to him.

As the crowds let loose their guttural chants as Chip began to sing, he knew what they knew. His voice brought people back from the edge. His voice rescued lost souls. His songs were their songs.

Chip was convinced his gift that he shared on most weekend nights, when asked, was a gift that elevated some and inspired all.

His vocal range, the depth of his libretto, the whole package was on display for one maybe two songs and then it was over, and another would take his place onstage. His gift would last maybe five minutes and then it was over; too soon for some, not long enough for others.

But while he was there, singing in that crowded bar, he was part of every one of them even as they yelled for him to get off the stage, citing time limits for karaoke singers.

Chip knew their faces and taunts didn't match what their hearts were saying. That was okay. They would get there.

He knew their laughter and boos were understandable and misplaced, maybe even misguided. He was a messenger of hope in a world of under-employment, increasing waistlines, and, of course, climate change.

After his first number, he looked around and found comfort that most of his inner circle had shown up to hear him sing, fellow accountants that had followed him for a while now.

For those and the others in the crowd who were getting closer and closer to the stage, maybe a little too close, the promise of half a pizza (meat lovers), breadsticks, and free soda refills inspired him to keep singing until told to stop or until someone ran out of quarters.

It was a tradition that quarters were thrown at some of the performers, and Chip usually got a pocket-and-a-half full of change after his performance, mostly in U.S. currency. Other things were thrown too, but he couldn't fit them in his pockets.

When Chip moved onto his second number, which was a slower, melancholic tune, he had to stop halfway through to validate what others were feeling in the room.

That's when he realized how careful he had to be amongst the company of so many who were vulnerable and suffering so much. He looked around the room in between verses and saw Clarisse.

A recent addition to his entourage, Clarisse was a new hire on the fourth-floor and specialized in an accounting specialty even more incredibly dry and boring than Chip's.

Clarisse was a poster child Zoomer. Despite being an accountant, she was an ardent socialist whose social causes included furry animals in a dozen countries that Chip didn't believe were real countries. He'd never heard of them and thought Clarisse was making up country names for dramatic effect.

But she was generally positive despite her political leanings and quickly got invited to a few and select social gigs that Chip and his tiny cohort went to ever so often.

She'd been hanging out with Chip and crew for a few weeks now, more out of morbid curiosity than anything else. She recently moved to the company headquarters from a satellite office that was even more crushingly lifeless and dull than her present one.

He hadn't figured her out yet, not completely. Everyone has an agenda, and he tried to look past what she had done to him a couple of weeks ago.

Despite what happened, there she was in the crowd, watching him sing, appearing to move slightly with the cadence and beat of the music and doing a good job of dodging things that were getting thrown at Chip.

It was only a couple of weeks ago on a Monday at work that, following a similar karaoke night the previous weekend, she pulled him to the side and into one of the fourth-floor conference rooms.

Time had flown since then, but Chip could remember that experience like it was yesterday. He was still trying to wrap his head around what she had done and why she was there at the karaoke bar now watching him sing.

Alone in the conference room with Chip that fated Monday morning, Clarisse dispensed with the niceties and asked him to put on headphones. She said she wanted him to listen to a familiar song from his karaoke list and sing along, out loud to her.

She was doing an experiment, she said, and wanted to collect some data. This wasn't the first time Chip had been rolled up and inserted into an unsanctioned science experiment, so he went with it.

It was a song he had sung just a couple of days ago at the bar. Clarisse came prepared. It was one of his favorites. *This will be easy*, Chip thought.

Clarisse brought a recording device and told him she wanted to record his voice and then reiterated that she was doing this for her niece and then said something else at a deliberately low volume as if she didn't want Chip to hear the other stuff.

This wasn't the first time someone had tried to record his voice; except this time he had given tacit permission by staying in the conference room. He would humor her but only this once.

He sighed, then smiled, then sighed again, and made her promise not to send out the recording for commercial reasons.

He put on the headphones, careful to practice some deep breathing and a few vocal workups before the song would come on and it would be game time.

The song was queued up and started playing. Chip cleared his throat again, took his queue, and began to sing with headphones on, in a conference room, with Clarisse looking on.

Why not, he thought. He did what he did for others, not for himself. Clarisse kept the same expression the entire time. She might have blinked once.

When the number was over and Chip took a sip from his bottled water, Clarisse asked Chip to wait a few minutes while she queued up the recording for him to listen.

As she played it back to him, Chip smiled inwardly while Clarisse looked intently into his eyes. He thought this was a little awkward.

She played Chip's recording for about a minute and then stopped the tape and took a small breath. Chip took one too.

Getting compliments in a group setting was a whole lot easier than getting them from just the one – too intimate, too familiar. He preferred social distancing when it came to his performances.

Clarisse was direct and to the point. She told him he lacked talent, pure and simple, and should try golf or pickleball, given his age. She said he was undoubtedly the worst singer on or off social media, which was saying something since she was a digital native and had grown up in that world.

Chip was expecting an entirely different reaction. He didn't get it. He didn't get Clarisse.

Clarisse, sweet Clarisse. This went on for a further two minutes as she tried to convince Chip to forsake his talent and give up on karaoke singing. "Please stop embarrassing yourself," she pleaded.

She was worried about him. She didn't want him to keep going under this illusion that he had talent, that he had a gift. There was no talent and no gift.

She assured him, with a tear forming in her right eye, that she would be his friend regardless of whether others unfriended him or not. Chip was taken back – his inner circle had been compromised.

How could Clarisse, someone he had taken under his wing, choose to accuse him, slander him, and denigrate him?

Chip looked at her for more than a moment that morning in the conference room and tried to say some comforting words to someone clearly conflicted and misguided. *She must be unhappy with her life*, Chip thought. It was the only logical conclusion to all of this.

This must be some sort of a warped cry for help than a well-intentioned critique, he reasoned. Chip sighed again. This time, she heard him.

Now, back onstage and in the middle of one of his favorite numbers, Chip saw Clarisse in the crowd, with a look of what looked like pity toward him. Maybe she was the one feeling pitiful?

What was her end game? He would keep her close until he really figured out what was going on with her.

Chip finished up his second number and gratefully accepted guacamole dip from a fan who was doubling as a waitress.

Monday. October 1st

Karaoke night took care of Saturday, and long walks and a classic western movie swallowed up Sunday. Now, Monday was here.

The drive to the doctor's office took ten minutes. The building was a modern medical office complex. The building was gray with dark, tinted windows.

He entered through the revolving door and walked straight to the elevator – also gray with dark, tinted windows. It was like the building held secrets and wouldn't let them out.

In less time than it took to spell optometry, he was in the doctor's reception area and signing in on the roster using a pen with incredibly colored feathers on the end.

Chip guessed they had had a problem with people stealing their pens in the past and had adopted extreme measures to improve pen retention. Thus, the feathers.

"Hi, my name is Chip Clementine. I have an appointment at 10 a.m. with Doctor Raj," Chip said cautiously to the unnamed twenty-something receptionist that didn't want to be there.

Her eyes slowly registered the new arrival but everything else about her said, "They don't let me out for lunch." Then the spark was lit.

"You're kidding, right?" her eyes came alive. She sat up in her chair, her smartphone fell off her lap onto the carpet.

She'd been watching downloaded episodes of a survivalist show on her phone carefully placed right below the counter and invisible to patients.

The internet was terrible in the office and live streaming was unreliable – thus the downloads. She was addicted to anything to do with Alaska, especially Alaskan survival shows.

"Sorry, what do you mean?" Chip said.

"Your name, Clementine. So cool! I wish I had a last name like that." *Finally, someone remotely interesting*, she thought.

"I wish my last name was mango or pomegranate," she said. Such energy, such interest!

Oh no, it's happening again, Chip thought.

He'd seen this before. He couldn't remember how many times young women, young enough to be his daughter's age, had commented on his name.

He thought after he left his thirties and forties that the flirting would stop. He couldn't get away from it. He even dressed down and roughed up whatever was left of his hair when he knew he would be in these types of situations, although this happening at a medical appointment took even him off guard.

He needed to shut this down and fast.

"Yes, um, thanks. I need to see Doctor Raj please."

Chip didn't smile; that only sent the wrong signal. *Let's keep this professional*, he thought to himself.

He knew that for both their sakes, the focus had to be on the appointment and not his name – that's how things went sideways in a hurry. Fortunately, his direct tone and simplicity of request snapped her back from idol worship.

"Did you say Doctor Raj?" She went back to work mode. Her next episode on her phone just started – automatic play feature. Her Bluetooth headset was telling her so. Where did she put her phone? she thought in rising panic mode.

"He's running a little late, should only be another few minutes." She picked up her smartphone from the floor. Whew!

Chip saw her change and thanked the iPhone for being the distraction he needed. *That was easier than most*, he thought to himself.

He took his seat next to the seawater aquarium that took up most of the lounge area. The aquarium was in the middle of the lounge, so if you didn't like fish or like to see anything aquatic, you were already starting off on the wrong foot.

Aquariums were meant to be soothing and calm. Not for Chip. His hands were clammy, just like the fish.

In a few moments, he would get his biopsy results, a biopsy taken from the strangest of places.

A few weeks ago, he noticed an abnormality in his right breast after a semi-hard workout at the gym and then confirmed when he showered back at home. In the shower, he felt the lump and it got him worried.

He surmised that it was probably a pulled pectoral muscle – nothing crazy, just something that can happen at a gym when you attempt to bench more than your body weight in front of your giggly accountant friends. It happened so fast.

When he lifted the weights, he felt a pop and a snap and thought this was it, albeit a glorious way to go, lifting weights and all. A week later, he got his first appointment with Doctor Raj who had immediately taken a biopsy sample and sent it off to the lab.

It didn't feel like it was going to be a congratulatory call. After a few minutes of staring at bright-colored, bloated Asian fish, Chip was called into Doctor Raj's office. As Chip walked in, he started to twitch, a butt twitch this time which only happened when he felt like he had no other options.

"Hi, Chip, take a seat," said Doctor Raj clinically, saying it like he gave the same detached welcome to everyone who walked through his door.

"Is this bad?" said Chip nervously. He didn't wait for an answer.

"How long have we known each other?" said Chip, clearly intended to go somewhere with this line of inquiry.

Doctor Raj answered with no emotion, "Since tenth grade."

"You still owe me, Raj."

Chip didn't have to say it but felt Raj needed reminding every so often. This was the so often.

Doctor Raj continued with the poker face.

"We got the results back. And, no, I don't owe you," said Raj. Doctor Raj had moved on with his life and owed nobody anything.

"Right breast?" said Chip with nowhere near the confidence of Doctor Raj, but taller nonetheless.

"Right…The biopsy showed some malignant cancer-like presence. We will need to do an MRI scan to see if and how much the spread is, but I think we are looking at a localized growth area."

"We can…" his voice trailed off, the first sign that he had reached a natural pause in the conversation. Natural pauses were common in his line of work.

"I have breast cancer!" Chip said in a rising voice and an accelerating pulse. He was heavy breathing now.

"Steady, Chip." Doctor Raj found over the years that the word 'steady' was a better word than some others he had used in the past like 'calm down' or, worse, 'relax.' Saying relax always solicited the opposite response in others.

"Yes, you do have breast cancer and, from what we can tell, it is probably localized and hasn't spread anywhere. But we'll schedule you in for a routine scan to confirm." Doctor Raj was distracted by an email that came in on his screen. Apparently, he was the winner of the office pool for the week – Go Steelers!

"Days or weeks?" Chip's eyes were bulging and he still had the iron grip on his chair.

Doctor Raj snapped back from his screen, feeling slightly guilty for not being present.

"I don't think you have to worry about that kind of a timeframe," Doctor Raj said, trying to project positivity, but these things were always so precarious. He saw this going down next either one of two ways. He kept going like he did so many times before.

"Look, Chip. I know this is a lot to take in, but we've caught this pretty early. The success rate for beating this is very high. I'm not that concerned and you shouldn't be either."

Chip wasn't listening.

"It's worse than I thought…do I have till next week?"

Chip was off the chair now, on his knees, and holding onto one of the chair legs, looking up at a seated Raj, with a nature frame of somewhere out west in the background, probably Utah. Chip didn't care how this looked.

"No, what I meant is that, after this scan, we should be able to treat this with chemotherapy. If the scan shows what I think it will show, this is very treatable. We should be able to shrink this to a negligible level."

Doctor Raj kept going. He had to. His next appointment was an older friend than Chip and it was an easier appointment than this one.

"I'll set you up with the sessions and some scheduled MRI exams and will see you in a month or so."

This was the queue when most people got up from off the floor, walked out stunned, made their appointment, and went home. Not Chip, not yet.

"How long do I have? Months or years?" Chip's grip had loosened from the chair leg but not much.

"Listen, Chip. We'll get you set up with the scan and then some chemotherapy just to be safe. That should do the trick. I've seen much worse. You really don't need to work yourself up," Doctor Raj said, standing up with a forced smile.

Chip's back was now on the rug with feet vertical against the sidewall. He felt like he could take cancer news somehow better if he could get feel the strength of the floor beneath him, although the wooden floors were a little creaky.

He looked pathetically up at the authority figure in the room. "I don't get it. I didn't know a man could get breast cancer. Is that even a thing?"

Chip didn't care how he looked. Okay, maybe a little.

"Yes, this is a little unusual. But men do get breast cancer."

Doctor Raj was down on the floor with Chip now, laying opposite each other. Doctor Raj wasn't used to be eye level with his patients, especially in the prone position. His wife told him he needed to work on his bedside manner so thought he would give this a try.

It seemed to help. Chip took a few deep breaths and sat up, giving himself a shake. *Wow, it worked*, Doctor Raj thought.

The walk back to the reception area was a blur for Chip, but he did remember getting lost and a nurse walking with him through the right swing doors this time.

Back with the wilderness-watching receptionists, there was some calendar checking, a few medical acronyms, and three forms to fill out. Forms calmed him a little. Forms were his friends.

He wasn't going to go back home after such news. He had cancer! He needed to go back to work, to his cubicle, to regroup, and then reach out to his inner circle as soon as possible.

If he went home, he knew he wouldn't engage with anyone, not even Mrs. Clementine.

He would collapse on the couch and order pizza. Telling his wife about the office visit could wait till later.

When he got back to work, there was a full-blown staff meeting in progress. The subject? Budget cuts.

There was enough commotion to distract and divert him just enough from his recent news.

Chip fell right back into worker bee and cubicle occupant on the fourth-floor, keen to see what was going on.

Why didn't I see the invite? Nothing like an emergency meeting to sharpen the mind.

Chapter 8
Telling People

In corporate America, meetings are routine and dry, barely registering on the excitement meter. Anyone daring to call a meeting an 'emergency meeting' was really putting their reputation on the line. Unless we were talking about accountants, then every meeting was an emergency.

In Chip's world, emergency meetings happened every day but were not really emergencies at all, like, let's say, the kind of emergency meetings doctors would have when a life was in the balance or a military leader would have with the troops pinned down under enemy fire.

Accountants slept easy at night because their definition of an emergency meeting fitted them quite nicely.

Accountants liked to call anything out of the ordinary an emergency. And nothing to an accountant screamed emergency meeting like having a meeting involving potential budget cuts. Now that was an emergency of the highest order.

If someone was to do a study on which group (i.e. accounting, marketing, procurement, finance, sales, etc.) called emergency meetings most often in an office; accountants would beat out the rest of the competition handily. It wouldn't even be close.

If pressed, they would confidently say every single emergency meeting had been worthy of all the hype…because it involved accountants who were the elite of those that most in the industry called 'back office' staff.

In corporate America, you're either front office or back office. There are only two camps. Front-office workers bring money in – they are the front lines, the hunters, the meat-eaters.

Back-office workers are way, way in the background. They support those that sweat in the arena of life, corporate life, making money for the company.

Back-office workers pride themselves on keeping things moving behind the scenes while others get the glory. You can guess who accountants were and, more easily, who they were not.

Back-office is summed up as all the unsexy things that happen at a company – think human resources, purchasing, marketing, and the mother of all back-office functions – accounting.

Accountants considered the back-office worker the real hero of the corporate world – the quiet professionals who never sought after praise despite keeping everything afloat and balanced.

Chip was back-office through and through and considered getting a tattoo…but only with a coupon.

He was tempted once, right after he passed his accountancy exams, but it turned out tattoo parlors don't really do coupons or discounts, at least where he lives.

Chip couldn't pay the full price for getting inked. Mrs. Clementine wouldn't let him, so he got a henna tattoo instead – a calculator and a ledger encircled by a large dollar sign.

It was quite beautiful but lasted only a week before fading out – Chip liked long baths, and long baths and henna tattoos don't go well together.

Chip was not only an accountant but he was a specialized accountant at that, with special training in the nuances of financial ledgers, reports, and other minutia that most accountants hoped other accountants would do and not them.

Chip was happy, even ecstatic to take on the driest, dullest tasks at work that required a level of conscientiousness and technical no-know that most simply didn't have or care to have.

He signed up for all of the usual accounting conferences and chimed in on several online chat forums to abreast on the latest changes in accounting law and policies.

At the larger venues, considered mandatory training for accountants to maintain their certification, Chip would opt to stay longer to participate in some of the spin-off sessions that took dull and boring to a new level, cementing his nerdiest of nerd's status on the fourth-floor as an accountant's accountant.

Because of his specialty, people only brought questions to him nobody else could or would answer. So, people generally left him alone.

Only he initiated or volunteered information (rare)…but he always maintained control. If he had nothing else, he had control, and part of being in control was choosing the time and place he would share his cancer diagnosis with those near and dear to him.

The first person he saw coming out of the elevator was a friendly face and an endearing name boot.

Chip spotted Jimbo across the breakroom where the staff was assembled for the meeting. Jimbo was a lifeline in a sea of confusion right now. Chip needed to tell him his news, but there were too many faceless forms (he forgot his glasses) holding coffee cups and jostling for position.

He didn't think he could get to him in time before this meeting would start. The boss stood up from his chair, took a deep breath and looked around. This was his first big meeting as a newly-hired manager and only just recently graduated from business school with an MBA and an attitude.

Barely one month into his new job, his time had come to shine, and he was not going to fail. He had prepared, rehearsed, and even dressed for this event. It was times like this when others would look to their leader (him) to take them through this crisis.

"Okay, settle down. Well, things aren't looking too good, folks. The front office is telling us we're not making our numbers."

He had read somewhere that saying 'folks' made him more approachable. Of course, that only worked on a few of the 'folks' in the room, mainly the older crowd that was near retirement and couldn't care less what any manager would say in any meeting.

Meetings for them were reasons to catch up with other 'folks' they hadn't seen in a while. It was a big company so when meetings like this happened it was a thing.

Most saw the boss for what he was – another aloof, distant, calculating, opportunistic manager fresh from B-school out to make a mark in his first rung on the corporate ladder.

He paused for effect, but it didn't do any good. He could see it in their eyes. He kept going like he was reading from a script which he was because he had the notecards, typed notecards with lots of underlines and exclamation points – prompts for someone that needed to be prompted.

Chip had never seen a manager with typed notes on notecards and Chip had seen his share of new managers come and go over the years. *Impressive*, Chip thought. The boss cleared his throat.

"So…I know we're accountants and don't do any of the selling, but we can always cut expenses and help out with trimming the bottom line. So, I need each of you to put your good idea hats on and shout out some ways we can save money for the company. Who wants to start?"

The boss had his assistant near him with a magic marker and a whiteboard. She was there to capture all of the good ideas and make sure the boss got credit for all of them.

Chip's nameless boss scanned the crowd. There was a long, long pause – *too long*, the boss thought. Chip wasn't surprised. This late in the afternoon, with post-lunch fatigue setting in, there would be no good idea hats to be found in this group. Ideas were always in short supply with accountants after lunch.

Then a voice penetrated the auditorium. "Cut the air conditioning!"

Chip said it out loud without thinking. Sometimes, he couldn't tell if he had used his outside voice or inside voice. This should have been his inside voice. It wasn't, it so wasn't.

"Who said that?" the boss said. The rest of the auditorium reacted with a steadily increasing volume of boos, hisses, and wailings. The crowd's reaction took Chip back a little, but he was ready for them.

Chip always thought the company could save money through better climate-control practices and he was ready for anyone to challenge him on it. Chip always had ideas, unusual for a middle-aged accountant with no prospects for advancement.

"Me, Chip Clementine – Accounting, fourth floor."

He said it slowly because when he said 'accounting' slowly, everyone who wasn't an accountant automatically thought what had been said by that person was beyond reproach and of the highest fidelity. They were accountants after all – the stewards of the company's innermost secrets and guardians of the corporate keep.

He didn't have to say which department or what floor; everyone knew Chip was an accountant and they were on the fourth floor. Some wished they weren't. Not Chip. He was a die-hard fourth floorer.

"Surely the air conditioning won't get cut," they whispered. Heads turned left, right, up, and down. Some heads turned all the way around and then back again.

A woman in the back of the auditorium fainted but no one bothered to help. Sally had a history of fake fainting. She'd fake fainted before and most thought this was another attention-getting move for all the wrong reasons.

So, ignoring Sally, they waited for what the boss would say next.

"Chip, I need serious ideas. Anyone else?" The boss was hoping for participation but not the kind that came from Chip. That was just nuts. Cutting the air-conditioning was not the kind of suggestion he could work with.

Without permission, his assistant wrote the words 'CUT A/C' in big, bold, blue letters on the whiteboard. The assistant had great penmanship and didn't make the rookie move of using the wrong colors to write with. Even the folks in the very back of the auditorium could see it.

The boss turned around and saw what she'd done but couldn't tell her to erase it. It was too late for that. The genie was out of the bottle. The notecards had outlived their usefulness. He was on his own now.

"Come on, people! I'm not kidding. Do you think I enjoy these meetings?" Chip heard giggles off to the right, and so did Peter, the boss who was now named.

It was clear who was really in charge and it wasn't the guy standing next to a portable whiteboard with an assistant. Chip piped up again, "Peter, if you are serious about saving, then cutting the air conditioning is the only way to make an impact."

Chip knew the game he was playing. Peter didn't like to be called Peter either. Peter was his first name but preferred his middle name.

Most people didn't address him by his first or middle name. They preferred no name, just his title – it made things easier for them when lines were drawn between management and the workers.

"Okay, I get it," Peter said, trying to sound confident. Peter didn't get it. Peter continued, "That's a little extreme, but thanks for your input, Chip. Any other ideas?"

Total silence. Peter's palms were getting sticky and he wondered if anyone could see his right eye twitch.

Meanwhile, most thought that with Peter's dismissal of Chip's idea, such an extreme measure was off the table. *Crisis averted*! they thought. Keeping the air conditioning meant they would enjoy a constant 68 degrees while surfing the net in their tiny cubicles. Life would go on uninterrupted.

Surely, they thought, someone else would offer up another more-acceptable solution. But it was to be Chip would offer up yet another bombshell. He was really enjoying this.

"Hey, Boss. I guess we could ration the staples."

Shrieks, gasps, and a few expletives.

"Is he serious?" they whispered. "He's joking! He's not joking!" someone yelled out.

One poor soul groaned "I like my stapler!" Someone else let out a half-hearted 'I second' like this was a parliamentary procedure with votes and quorums.

The man who did the seconding had feeling in his voice but lacked sufficient bass to carry the day, so it sounded more like a plea than a statement. His 15 minutes of fame had been condensed to five seconds. That was all he would get – the famous seconder who tried to keep everyone's stapler. All eyes went from the 'I second' guy quickly to the boss.

Peter knew Chip's second idea was the one that would carry the day. Chip knew it too. If he had started out with the stapler plan it wouldn't have carried. Chip needed something extreme to soften the crowd up – cutting the air-conditioning elicited the right response and set the right conditions.

Peter, on the other hand, was conflicted. He didn't know how he was going to sell reduced staples to management as the fourth floor's answer to budget cuts. Seemed petty and not terribly impactful. He had no choice.There was an audible sigh from Peter, followed by slumped shoulders and the lowering of eyes. So much for his big debut. His assistant had already left.

"Go on," Peter said dejectedly and now utterly alone."Everyone can keep their stapler," Chip was careful with his tone. He wanted to come across as selfless rather than self-serving. It was important for him to be seen as the reluctant hero.

By this time, he had casually moved up to the front and was standing next to Peter. Peter was taller, but Chip seemed somehow the one in charge.

Chip continued, "I'm talking about staples, not staplers. I guess," he said it like he didn't want to do it, but, of course, he did.

"I can set up a distribution point and ration out individual staples on an as-needed basis and with proper documentation. This will save us a bunch!"

"I second the motion!" this time, someone said it with passion…and bass, not like the earlier seconder. Jimbo could always be counted on at the most pivotal point.

"This isn't a democracy," Peter said in a losing voice, but he gave it one last try.

"We don't vote here! I'm the boss!" The last statement was barely audible. It was more like he was saying it to himself and not to others.

Maybe what he really needed to hear was that someone had faith in him, but at that moment, only he could give himself the validation he needed.

Peter knew he was close to losing everything. He had to put his stamp on things. It was getting close to lunchtime.

"Okay, Chip. Let's give this one a try."

Everyone turned to Chip. Chip was slightly flushed, but it never got in the way of what he needed to say when he needed to say it.

"Peter – look, this is easy. I'll set up the staples supply by my cubicle. All I ask is that you (pointing to Peter for visual effect) back me up if others get their feelings hurt when requests are occasionally denied."

Everyone knew there had been a change in the room – Chip was taking over. Peter knew it too so did what he knew he had no other choice to do.

"Done," he said in a beaten voice. Peter looked up from the floor and scanned the crowd for support but got nothing.

In a much lower voice than he started out with, he said, "Thanks, everyone – good meeting." Then Peter melted back into the crowd and faded into the background. He would report back to his leadership a rosy and highly skewed picture of how everything had gone down.

Later, his assistant typed up the brief minutes of the meeting and Peter molded and bent the words to show how he solicited quality input to address a real problem. He didn't mention Chip.

***

When the meeting broke up, Chip headed back to his cubicle area and saw his friends talking up a storm near the water cooler. They were in their usual place, positioned near the elevator but not so near that they looked like they were ready to bolt for lunch just yet, although it was getting close. They'd been in the same meeting as Chip but on the other side of the auditorium.

Chip struggled with how to join in on a group conversation without it being awkward. He had news to share, but when was the right moment?

In previous attempts to join a group conversation underway, he tried different things, different tactics, all to no avail. But he was really desperate to tell his friends, and because desperation is the mother of creativity, he considered a whole new range of options to join in on a group conversation without fanfare or fuss.

First, he could throw something (call it a diversion), but someone might see him and form an opinion that Chip was more eccentric than otherwise supposed.

Second, he could pay someone on the inside to bring him in with some clever, rehearsed remark that would get people nodding quickly while Chip moved to the center.

Third, he could act physically injured as if a random book or, more likely, a technical manual had fallen off the shelf on his head and medical attention was required.

The medical option was not always the best to do around other accountants who attempted the same thing before but for different reasons.

It was the fourth thought that went through Chip's mind that resonated and stuck.

Maybe, a few well-placed, low-grade explosives might get the job done more efficiently? That would break things up a bit and he would have a captive audience at least until security showed up, if you could call them security.

Chip thought this one through. Firecrackers properly timed would cause a commotion, and the smoke would activate the sprinkler system. This is where Chip would make his money.

He knew the manual shut-off valve to the sprinklers and would 'let it ride' for about two seconds (enough to get light dampness on one's clothing and panic to set in).

Chip would then shut the valve and join the group with the added bonus of looking like a hero. He would have their full attention. They would listen without distractions.

He would tell some elaborate story of how this thing had been going around lately and he's lucky he got to the sprinklers before the fire marshal was notified, an easy sell since nobody wanted that to happen.

There would be the usual expressions of gratitude, maybe some hugs. Chip knew there were only so many times this would work, but the risk was worth the reward.

In the end, he tried none of the options. Clear thinking prevailed as it had done so many times before, and he opted for trusting that others would give him his moment.

He greeted them with his secret accounting handshake and then said he had some tough news to share.

They took it in stride. They were accountants, so there was no emotion, just fixed stares and stronger grips on their water bottles, except Robin who had a wry smile on her face like she didn't believe him.

But most did squeeze the bottles. One of them, Rosslyn, had a throwaway bottle, so when she squeezed, it exploded. To her credit, she maintained the fixed stare with Chip, although it weakened in its intensity.

When asked how long he had to live (they were to the point like he was), he answered, "It's not long, friends." Chip never called them his friends, but now seemed like the right time. He could get some mileage out of this.

Still, this was tough (ish) news to share. For some other of his friends, it would have to be news delivered one-on-one. The question was how.

Eddie had not been in the group that day, so he would get the individual treatment. Telling Eddie had taken time, all day actually.

Eddie sat directly across from him, separated by three feet of space that included computer monitors and a small six-inch-high partition that hid prized electronic pencil sharpeners and a few mementos from their last cruise together.

They were close, and their wives got along which was a bonus. Sitting in his cubicle, he was thinking hard, too hard, about how to break it to Eddie.

His second-tier friends already knew from earlier in the day, but he knew Eddie wouldn't have heard about it from them.

Eddie kept to himself. And that was when Chip caught himself staring at Eddie from across their monitors.

Chip had to think of something quick; they often stared at each other while they thought about things.

"Hey, Eddie. Do you remember the other day when we were talking about our forever homes?"

Eddie was staring at Chip. No answer yet. Chip continued.

"Well, if I was building my forever home, I would also build an underground shelter," Chip said, knowing this would get Eddie's attention.

Underground shelters made Eddie's conversational starter shortlist every time.

Eddie snapped out of his trance. Something had clicked.

"You'll need a tunnel," he said.

"Of course," Chip said in a neutral tone.

"Actually, two tunnels. One would be an alternate."

"Why an alternate?" Chip asked. There was an audible sigh from Eddie.

"If you get overrun, you'll need an alternate way out."

There was nothing neutral in tone about Eddie's voice. He wasn't just mouthing the words, he meant them. "Overrun?" Eddie let out another long, audible sigh bordering on annoying.

"Yes," said Eddie.

Chip felt like he needed to clarify a few things.

"I'm talking about an underground shelter if we get hit by a tornado or hurricane or other large gale-force wind."

Chip thought the conversation had veered off somehow. Then Eddie showed his true colors.

"I'm talking about the undead breaking through your perimeter."

Eddie said undead like everyone else would say cucumber, mortgage, or balloons – things that were real, existed. The words hung in the air, unchallenged, for 13 seconds.

"Zombies don't exist, Eddie," Chip said. His eyebrows were raised.

Chip read somewhere that if you respond calmly when dealing with unpredictable people, you have a better-than-average chance of not getting pulled into the madness.

Chip spoke slowly in measured tones despite the raised eyebrows. He couldn't change those.

"That is what they'd have you believe," Eddie said.

"Who is 'they'?" Chip asked. Chip honestly didn't know.

"We should probably end this conversation. Others may be listening," Eddie said this last point quietly, then looked up at the ceiling like someone or something was observing them.

Eyes shifted back to respective screens. *It is either now or tomorrow*, Chip thought. *Here it goes.*

"Eddie, I have breast cancer."

"Yeah, right. Nice try," Eddie said. Now, Eddie's eyebrows were both up and twitching a little.

"I'm serious. I don't know how much longer I have," Chip said, wanting some emotional validation but knew it would be a reach with Eddie.

Raised eyebrows may be all that Chip was going to get from him.

"Guys don't get breast cancer – it's a statistical impossibility. You probably pulled a muscle when you tried that bench-press thing."

Eddie wasn't a jock either, so anything involving weightlifting or sweating was a thing.

Eddie was there that day when Chip had attempted to bench press half his body weight and it hadn't gone down well.

"Well, I thought that's what it was. But it turns out I need chemotherapy for this. I mean, I have to get a body scan first, but it's looking like I will have a round or two just to be safe or at least that's what Doctor Raj is thinking."

Doctor Raj was Eddie's doctor as well and had been since his own private cancer battle a few years ago, a battle Eddie never shared with Chip.

"Apparently, it's treatable, but you know, Eddie, I could be three weeks away from putting in my last sick leave request."

"Who've you told?" Eddie said, finally ungluing himself from his monitor, swiveling his chair around, and looking at Chip.

Eddie's eyes darted from left to right as if he could see through the partitioned walls behind Chip.

"Just you and the second-tier guys." That is what Eddie and Chip called them – they had their uses.

"Doesn't sound that serious, but this could be an opportunity for leverage," said Eddie, fully engaged and present with Chip.

Eddie's world was one-hundred percent negotiable, and leverage was his language, his currency.

"Leverage?" Chip asked.

"We can work this thing to our advantage. Is the Coupon Club on for Friday?"

"Yeah," Chip replied. Chip hoped Eddie could help him navigate through all of this. Turning a cancer diagnosis into a platform for personal gain was something even he had not envisioned just yet. Eddie had beaten him to it.

"I see possibilities with this. Let's strategize over pizza tonight at your house," Eddie said.

Strategize and pizza put together in the same sentence was code for Chip buying the pizza and Eddie finishing his ice cream in the garage freezer where the good stuff was kept.

Eddie fidgeted in his chair as if this news ignited some forward momentum in his life. He leaned forward slightly but not too much or vertigo would kick in.

Later that night, they talked, strategized, and ate pizza the way only two nerdy accountants can. With Eddie's help, Chip was able to see ways he could navigate through this new journey of his.

He hadn't realized before how creative (and devious) Eddie could be. He would bring in donuts on Monday and Eddie would be offered two of them as a thank you.

It was the least he could do after starting off October the way he had. Chip knew friends like Eddie could get him through this month of all months.

Cancer was scary, but scary with someone else like Eddie would always end up being doable – scary but doable.

Part 3
Getting on with It

Chapter 9

Making New Friends

Everything Was White. Everything.

The fluorescent lighting in the MRI room was so bright, it hurt his eyeballs. Chip wasn't used to this level of a reveal.

In the past couple of weeks, Doctor Raj had moved quickly on scheduling Chip for his mandatory MRI scan, the scan that would hopefully confirm some things and rule out others.

Chip waited patiently for this day, but now that it was here, he was nervous and jittery. Being half-naked didn't help either.

In his one-piece gown which flattered his left side but not the right, Chip was ready to take instructions from anyone if it speeded up the process a smidgen or even half of one.

The brightness was intense. Chip was enveloped in an unnatural glow of light that exposed him for what he was – scared and claustrophobic with a dash of jitters.

In that room, he felt like he was under a microscope. The whole room was the inner workings of a microscope. He was the lab rat.

In the center of the room was an all-white scanning machine with a cylindrical opening that would slide human beings in and out on a large metal tray. It was all so clinical and claustrophobic. There was probably 3D printing going on somewhere in the background, he thought, replicating me for another science experiment later in the day!

The last time Chip was in a hospital was the unfortunate incident with the blood drive when, despite his best efforts, he succumbed to his fears and said and did things he wished he could take back.

He thought he was over that episode and would be much stronger for it the next time he entered a medical facility. But that was before he stepped into this bad sci-fi movie set with the hard white plastic and metallic décor.

This was also before he realized that all the comforting talk he got from Jillian, the MRI technician, when he first showed up could not stop the onset of cold sweats and the spasms in his right leg.

When Jillian showed him around the room and before sending him to the changing room, he was careful to take in the surroundings. Outside the room, he could see people buzzing around with a calmness that unnerved him.

At his own office, there was chaos, some expletives, one or two emotional outbursts, and muffled sounds in the breakroom – and that was a Tuesday.

Here, in the sterile MRI room and outside, there was none of that. Jillian seemed so competent, so confident, so chill. Therefore, he didn't trust her. She was too staged and she looked like she just graduated high school.

Jillian must have been through this before with other patients, Chip thought. He could tell this was not her first go around, what, with the forced smile and non-medical language she used to ease Chip toward the sliding metal bed after he emerged from the changing, feeling vulnerable.

The bed was surprisingly comfortable when he laid on it, which made Chip uneasy. Things would have been easier if there was more metal and less fluff, fewer sheets, and pillows. The pillows seemed like a ruse, like someone was about to get played.

And he didn't need to feel the foam beneath him either, like that was going to smooth things over. He didn't need foam.

Everything was manipulation, a trap – a precursor for pain that was likely to come soon, masqueraded by clean, white sheets.

He was offered earplugs. He declined.

He was offered headphones with jazz. He refused out of principle but not because of the jazz.

For my first scan, I'll have the full experience, Chip thought. He could not have any sedatives, crutches, anything that would deaden his senses. But he would take the weighted blanket – that was a given.

He needed to be in full control if he was going to have to lay still for forty-five minutes while the machine did its scanning thing. He still hadn't told Jillian he was claustrophobic.

The first sign of trouble for Chip was what Jillian said innocently as he was sent sliding into the bowels of the metallic coffin with the foam and two fluffy pillows keeping his head in place.

Jillian maintained eye contact the whole time he was moving on the sophisticated conveyer belt.

"If you start to get panicky, just press the button and we'll get you out right away."

She spoke slowly and calmly which increased Chip's anxiety barometer a few notches.

Chip pressed the button out of instinct, multiple times, and with conviction – better to test out the gear before it's too late. Jillian gave him a wry smile and said something he didn't hear. Then he heard what she said next.

"Mr. Clementine, I can assure you the device works. There's no need to worry. I'm right here."

He pressed it again twice just to get a reaction. He got one – raised eyebrows and pursed lips. She was behind the glass partition, pushing buttons and recording what Chip was about to go through.

Chip was on his own. He was unable to move and only able to see so much through the bottom of his feet, which was limited to the blurry silhouette of Jillian tapping away on her phone with her extra-long artificial nails. That was when the shakes returned.

He knew it wasn't the cold, it was the adrenalin. He was trapped inside this metal monster and felt its weight bearing down on him like a lead blanket. The shakes continued.

The last round of shakes down his right leg had bounced the beeper out of his left hand, and he was left wondering if there was a God. He could see it but could not reach it.

The weighted blanket worked well, too well. He couldn't signal for help without that beeper. He would have to try something else.

According to Jillian, during her short orientation of the room, there was a small camera next to him to monitor his facial expressions in case of an emergency. He would try to contact her non-verbally. He thought it was his only shot.

He looked directly at the camera and mouthed his pleas for help.

He needed that beeper back to regain some control inside this metallic world. The beeper was gone and so were his inhibitions. He needed to act.

He wasn't sure anyone was monitoring the camera feed. Somehow, Chip wiggled his right arm from underneath the soul-crushingly heavy blanket.

He was in a white coffin the size of a hospital room, with only one loose arm to make a difference to anything.

His heart was racing, and his eyes were blinking uncontrollably. He needed to get attention. He needed someone in authority, a higher pay grade than Jillian, with her latest iPhone and fake concern for others.

His freed right arm reached up and around the side of the hollow tube. He only had so much reach and banging on the tube did nothing for the situation since no one could hear him.

He felt a cord and pulled it without thinking. His world of whiteness suddenly turned black.

Chip accidentally pulled a nearby power cord. This alerted Jillian who had looked at the monitor and then ran over to him, clearly out of breath and out of ideas and midstream in a texting war with her boyfriend. And, because it was pitch black, Chip could hear her banging her frame against his stretcher bed as she hit maximum velocity.

"Mr. Clementine, are you okay?" Jillian asked out of breath, although it was probably only about twenty feet between her monitoring station, or whatever she called it, and Chip.

She was nervous but kept talking.

"Something's happened. We've lost power and I can't get connectivity on my phone."

The emphasis on the phone was disconcerting. *How about the fact that we are without power, Jillian?* Chip thought, trying for a better way to politely question her priorities.

Jillian didn't ask him what had happened. She would never assume in a million years that one of her patients had shut down the place with the yank of a cord or two.

Chip knew instantly what happened or, more importantly, who had done it.

"I think I did it. I think I pulled that plug."

Chip was still holding it – he'd pulled it from wall.

"I was terrified, and you were too busy texting to help me. I had to do something." He felt the weight of what he did on his shoulders and a little bit on the back of his neck. He then pointed out the obvious.

"Jillian, other than your iPhone backlight, everything's black, and I've never felt comfortable in the dark."

He thought about putting on a brave face, but he was middle-aged and had given up trying to be someone he wasn't.

This is why he never went to the attic when he was a kid, too scary! Jillian wasn't listening to Chip. She had bigger problems to deal with.

"Please don't tell anyone about this. I would definitely lose my job. I can't handle another job change," Jillian said, clearly rattled by recent events.

"So, what happens next?" Chip asked.

"Well, I guess we just wait until the door access codes are rebooted and we can get out. Can you get out of the scanner?"

Jillian was thinking.

She knew there was a manual somewhere of what to do if the building loses power and the patient is strapped inside the MRI scanning machine, but she was barely awake during orientation and missed the part on where to find standard operating procedures for these kinds of things.

Chip was still entirely and utterly pressed down by that weighted blanket. Only his right arm free. So, Jillian relied on common sense.

"Mr. Clementine, if you can't get out of the scanner, since it's dark, maybe we should just stay still and wait for help. I hear voices in the corridor." She thought a little levity might help in the situation.

"Man. This is so episode one of Walking Dead, right?" Jillian exclaimed.

"Walking what?"

Chip didn't know what she was talking about. Chip wasn't the only one afraid of the dark.

Jillian grew up in a home where the bedroom night-light stayed on. This stemmed from a particularly bad storm years ago when she was eight years old and the storm knocked out the electricity in their cul-de-sac.

With no candles and no plan, she and her two sisters huddled in her parents' bedroom while her mom spoke soothing words and her dad tried to suppress his feelings of helplessness, another family member scared of the dark but too proud to admit it.

After that event, Dad had made sure all the rooms in the house had their own night light. But Jillian had never forgotten that night before the night lights were put in.

Years later, in that confined MRI, Jillian felt like she was a young girl again in her parents' house.

As her anxiety level rose, she needed something, anything to stay in control. She was, after all, the one with the security badge and hospital scrubs. This kind of thing wasn't discussed during the new employee orientation. She knew enough to know that her patient was counting on her to be calm.

She would be the first to make the overture. She didn't have long before she would fold mentally and retreat to a corner of the room. It was time to re-engage with Mr. Clementine, the middle-aged man who had single-handedly shut down the building.

"Mr. Clementine, we may be here for a while. Is this your first time at the clinic?" *Maybe conversation would be their salvation*, Jillian thought.

"Yes. Please call me Chip."

"So, what do you do for a living?" Jillian asked, trying to be casual.

"I'm an accountant. Well, technically I'm a cost accountant."

"Cost, what? What's an accountant?" Jillian barely passed her math classes, and accountant sounded like more math. She hoped he would say it wasn't anything to do with math.

"We do a lot of math," Chip said. It was easier to explain his job this way.

"I hate math. I'm more of an English major." *That was a lie*, Jillian thought, *I was never a major in anything.*

"What shows do you like to watch? T.V. shows?"

"I like science fiction and anything involving hoarders," Chip replied. It was a toss-up between the two, but either one would work when he needed to unwind.*Snap!* Jillian thought, *something in common.* Jillian saw an opening.

"You like science fiction? Awesome. Star Wars or Star Trek?"

"Star Trek, without a doubt." Chip was focusing more on Jillian than being strapped in his own private death machine. Why hadn't Jillian unstrapped him? Then he remembered, if he raised his head two inches, he would bump into the inside of the metallic coffin.

"What about the captains? Which one is your favorite, Picard or Kirk?" Jillian asked.

This was a start, Jillian thought. *If we don't keep talking, this is going to get really weird, really fast.*

"Picard, of course."

"Huh, if you were Kirk, we wouldn't be in the dark." Sometimes Jillian said out loud what she was thinking. This was one of those moments. The conversation went off trajectory.

"That's a little harsh, Jillian. There was an attic when I was younger. It was quiet and very dark. I got trapped up there, kind of like a Home Alone scene. My sister rescued me when she heard me screaming."

Chip felt he had been a little sharp himself so he would throw Jillian a bone.

"You're right about Captain Kirk though. I bet he never got trapped in an attic. Anyway, where are you going with this?"

"Sorry. All I'm saying is this is where you see the difference between a Kirk and a Picard. Kirk would operate in the dark as if nothing had happened. Picard would have insisted on lighting, makeup, and a cue card – he was such a diva."

"Diva? Picard? That man's a legend. Picard wouldn't have cancer in the first place – his mental will would have denied cancer a place in his body."

"Does cancer scare you, Chip?" Her question was genuine. Chip felt she really wanted to know.

"My doctor doesn't seem concerned. But it still stops you in your tracks when someone gives you the C-word.

"Most days, I do okay – I have friends at work and my wife supports me when she's home and not doing her real-estate thing. But some days, I feel lonely, like no one knows what I'm going through."

Jillian waited for the right moment.

"You know, there's a breast-cancer-support group that meets at the clinic every Wednesday night.

"They wear pink and have the most amazing food. They seem to have fun – laughing. Every once in a while, they have a movie night, but mostly they just sit around and chat."

Jillian was trying to be helpful. It was working.

"Are there any men in this support group, Jillian?" he asked another obvious question.

"No. But why not? Why can't men have breast cancer and talk about it with women, share their feelings, etc.? Since you like Picard so much, I could totally see Picard in one of those meetings. Kirk, not so much."

Chip didn't know how to answer that, but it sounded deep and the best thing he could manage was a squeeze of Jillian's hand and a long exhale.

She had been holding his hands the whole time and he hadn't known what to do except when the squeeze felt like the right thing.

The darkness became comfortable. It had been ten minutes and there were no signs of life outside the room from what he could tell, just quietness.

Chip felt there was a natural pause in their conversation when he saw the lights flicker on outside and then heard the intercom voice announce that main power was restored and that everyone should standby for clinic doors to be unlocked.

Within seconds, blinding fluorescence light flooded the room.

They stared at each other, one on the stretcher slab and the other on a small chair nearby, holding each other's hands. They broke. They'd been through something special, sharing a bit of themselves with the other in the dark.

When a supervisor arrived, Jillian brushed his questions aside and focused on her patient. Now that she could see him, she took off the EKG plugs suctioned on Chip, refusing to answer questions until she was done.

One or two pulled plugs emitted whimpers from Chip, but he didn't care. *Jillian gets me*, he thought.

When the all-clear was given, Chip quickly got dressed and left through the side entrance. The firefighters had been there for a while in the main lobby, and building security was not finished interviewing people. Jillian was whisked upstairs for a more formal inquiry.

Chip didn't want to be questioned for understandable reasons. If they got to him, he knew he had an ally in Jillian. She would cover for him.

Chip left the building with one more friend in the world. He was going to look into support-group meetings at some point in the future.

He thought there was one that met at work, afterhours in the cafeteria. But the more he thought about meeting with strangers about something so personal like this, he wasn't so sure.

He wasn't ready just yet. Maybe later, but not now.

Chapter 10
Stress Relief

It was the last Friday in October, almost four weeks since Chip's diagnosis and a couple of weeks since the meltdown in the MRI room. Chip was reflecting and Fridays were as good a time as any to reflect.

Friday afternoons were a gift from the heavens – a time to ease back on the pace, forget about cancer, power down and turn inward. Incoming calls and emails would find no joy or closure, at least not until Monday; Tuesday was more likely.

Requests from management would go unanswered at best or rejected at worst. Mail would stack up, unread, and spill over into Eddie's workspace, Chip's cubicle neighbor who didn't mind the spillage as long as there were no liquid containers involved.

Eddie didn't know what an in-box was or how it got there. But Eddie, like Chip, knew Fridays were part-reflecting and part-coupon club gatherings.

Chip and Eddie knew what they would be doing later on in the afternoon and it started with coupon and ended with club. Today was going to be his lucky day. Coupon Club!

As with other Friday afternoons at 3 p.m., Chip and the rest who were vetted cast off thoughts of work and assembled in the breakroom with their cut-out coupons and some loose change.

It was time for the Coupon Club to meet!

The rules were simple. Arrive with at least ten discount food or clothing-related coupons that can be used locally. Each coupon had to offer at least 50 percent or more off as a discount. Those 'two for one' or 'buy one get one free' deals didn't count, as most in the group didn't appreciate the math involved.

Anyone possessing fast-food coupons would face disciplinary action, as possessing such coupons was grounds for dismissal from the club or two weeks' suspension.

Most people took the suspension rather than make a fuss and flame out of the club on a principle or two.

No one enforced the rules, but there was typing in the background when a faux-pas was committed. There were so many coupons that were collected, cut, and sorted for this event.

There was a division of labor so that no one showed up with the same coupons. That happened only once in the past six months and it had not turned out so well for Jen – poor Jen. To be banished from this club is to lose a part of your soul.

This was also a barter system in effect. Each started out as equals under club rules, but some in the group quickly rose to the top – their high-pitched screams for one coupon or the other, followed by thrown objects from nearby desks was bizarre but effective.

In the end, some bartered their way to a treasure trove of bargains while others lost everything. This system rewarded risk and punished complacency.

Chip's record was respectable. He'd found an 80% off coupon from a local clothing store this week, but it cost him dearly and not in dollars and cents. He was still shaken by the experience and still looked over his shoulder when sporting goods coupons were brought up.

No one ever voluntarily left the club – some tried but they were half-hearted attempts.

Once you joined, it was for life or until you had something better to do on a Friday afternoon at work.

As Chip looked around the breakroom amidst the screaming, the scissors, and the paper, he knew he'd found his home away from home. Sure, it was a dysfunctional family with the usual drama, but it was real, and they knew it was real.

He could no more separate himself from the club and his coupon-cutting friends than he could misfile a quarterly report or answer his phone with a fictitious name and a foreign accent. This was his second home but without a mortgage.

When Chip casually brought up his diagnosis around the table, he thought everyone would have known by then. He was wrong, utterly, epically wrong.

The few who didn't know reacted predictably – they went through the seven stages of grief in less than three minutes – shock, denial, anger, rationalization, acceptance, etc. Some were more understanding than others. One or two had to be picked up from the floor.

Chip, Eddie, and a few others clipped away amidst the shrieks, the whimpers, the hugs – it was all too much. Act like it was no big deal, they thought to themselves.

Most had taken only one anxiety pill to get them through the day. This revelation was cause for a second, but it was nowhere to be found. So, some decided to suffer in silence.

That was when Chip decided he needed to do what others did when they got cancer.

As Chip looked around, he didn't want to be like so many he saw, figuratively lying there and accepting one's lot in life.

He wanted to challenge his fate; nothing was pre-ordained.

He would do some things differently, extroverted things. He would take risks, make new friends. He also was badly in need of expanding his social circle, he thought.

He would later say that the coupon club was the place where he plotted a new course for himself, one that would get him a little more out of his shell, push a few boundaries, and reassess some relationships that had been stuck on neutral for a while.

***

The following week was a rebound week. The last one had been quite a doozy, and he wanted this week to be uneventful and unremarkable while he had time to think about creating a cancer-fighting bucket list or two.

Late in the afternoon, he was surprised to see a few of his colleagues that he usually didn't see until at least Thursdays after they had gone through their number crunch period and circulated around the office. They needed a breather, they would say, and they took their breaks together but only on Thursdays.

Chip didn't get why they were there – it was a Wednesday. Something was up.

He became more suspicious when they greeted him with pleasantries and accolades for something he had done earlier last month. These colleagues were renowned for a) not being pleasant and b) not complimenting anyone, ever. Something was up.

He called them out on it and they came clean.

They had spoken with each other beforehand and were there to have an 'intervention' with Chip.

Chip had been in on other interventions and considered it relationship building, something all could get something out of, including the interveners.

Chip could not, for the life of him, figure out why, this time, it was his turn to be the intervenee.

Chip's obsession with Christmas light decorations was the reason for the intervention. What others called obsession, Chip called festive celebrations.

Chip's festive celebrations started in early November, about a month before anyone else on the fourth-floor, in the building, and before anyone else in the country even thought about putting up Christmas lights and decorating their cubicle with all things Christmas.

The intervention group had talked about nothing else when Chip put up his array of blinking Christmas lights on the first day of the month that should have been focused on Thanksgiving. They needed to shut this thing down. It wasn't healthy.

If Chip had a weakness, he was a pushover for all things Christmas. He loved the season and December, his birthday month. He decorated his desk with fake holly garland and Christmas cards from yesteryear. He never threw anything away. It was all reusable; not recyclable, just reusable.

He had two stockings in prominent view (one for him, one for anyone else that would agree to be his holiday buddy).

And, then there was candy. Free peppermint mints to sweeten the pot. Any takers?

But his signature statement was, without doubt, his 50-foot-long blinking Christmas lights that surrounded his six-foot by nine-foot cubicle, not once but twice over.

All colors on the spectrum were represented and were especially bright because Chip had removed all overhead fluorescent lighting in the area...permanently. Permanently meant off until Chip turned them back on which was not until mid to late January, depending on his mood.

The group had planned this intervention carefully.

First, Chip was asked politely to remain in his seat without comfort food. Each person told Chip how they suffered from those blinking lights over the last four days since they had been turned on. One of them, in tears, said they couldn't have any festive lights at their house – it reminded them of work. His kids thought he was the worst dad ever. His wife agreed with them.

Their argument was also that not everyone is emotionally ready for Christmas, it being early November and all. They wanted to squeeze a little more out of fall.

They complained of power surges on their computers, flickering monitoring screens that were synchronized with his 'freaking' lights, and how each time they passed his desk, they suffered momentary blindness from the visual displays.

Two in the group described how the lights reminded them of past roadside accidents at night, all involving random imagery and, of course, blinking lights.

Everyone had suffered in different ways and wanted Chip to validate them – he wouldn't.

They wanted him to pull that plug and 'shut down those lights, Chip!' He couldn't.

They gave him more time to change his answer – thirty seconds (with a timer) to process, reflect, and commit to pulling the plug. He didn't need thirty seconds.

What he needed was five seconds to steel himself, clear his throat, and state in a loud voice a few choice words.

"I will not shut down my lights – not for you, this office, or this company – you need these lights as much as I do. Come on, people. It's Christmas time!" And then there was the *pièce de résistance*.

"You do know I have cancer, right!?" He was hoping others within earshot would hear him and break this thing up.

They heard him but had turned the volume up on their headsets as a way to retreat rather than rush to another's aid. The timer kept timing away, but it was no use. Another wasted prop.

Chip wouldn't budge, not with that state declaratory statement.

When the timer went off, Chip was there staring them down with his eye twitch. Chip was going to keep his Christmas lights up whether they liked it or not, whether the lights triggered their own memories or not. Nothing rose to the level to beat out an 'I have cancer' statement.

He knew that this year more than others, he had the best chance to keep going with the lights.

It's not like this didn't happen every year – it did. They would try again next year, maybe with the addition of more forceful voices. Maybe a few in their group would be politely excused – they needed lions, not lambs for this type of gig.

And then it was over. Another failed intervention.

Chip knew what this meant for the rest of November as the others walked away, back to their cubicles without holiday spirit. Chip knew this wouldn't be over. Other groups were forming all the time with the same gripes.

There would be lingering resentment for the rest of the month and into the next.

He would have to be extra vigilant against those that would do him (actually his lights) harm.

It was decided; he would install his own nanny came to watch over the lights. A drone was a bit much, so he settled for a fixed camera rather than a roving one.

A little extreme, yes. Totally appropriate given the risk, absolutely.

Until they were all sent home for Christmas holiday break, he would monitor his blessed lights remotely like a concerned parent would for their infant.

He would be their protector. He would do this for himself and the lights, but he would also do it for the others that he thought secretly needed his little, colored beacons of light and hope.

If anyone attempted to move the lights, he would play back the recorded video as a learning moment for some and an indictment for others.

No one ever told him words to that effect, but it made no difference. His supporters were out there, somewhere.

Chip had other questions too as he replayed the intervention in his mind over and over again.

Chip prepared himself for a night away from home and broke out the sleeping bag.

The security guard came by to check on him after everyone had left, and Chip settled in for the first of many nights, fighting for a cause but at odds with a less-than-understanding spouse.

Chapter 11

The Bucket List

Several weeks had passed since the diagnosis. He dealt with it largely on his own with no outside help. There weren't any cancer-support group meetings on Chip's calendar just yet. He didn't think he was ready for that kind of support or therapy yet. But he did think about his cancer more as he got closer to Christmas.

His chemotherapy treatment was scheduled for right after the holidays in early January. He knew his cancer wasn't a death sentence and he would probably get through it, but he still felt that he should be doing something more with his life than just thinking about his next chemo treatment.

He needed to prove some things to himself and others, mostly others. He would put together a list of things he should do and get moving on his own steam before the Christmas holidays.

He had to start living his life on his terms, not something else's. He would put together a bucket list of things he would want to do before he couldn't or wouldn't.

His bucket list was written shorthand, quickly, and with twitchy handwriting. The more he thought about what he wanted to do, the faster he wrote, unrestrained.

This was his chance to dare, to dream, to soar. So item #1 on his list had been scribbled nervously.

'FLASH MOB (by Christmas)'

There, the words had been penned. There was truly something he would never do in his lifetime unless pushed and pushed hard.

He had dreamed about it for the past decade. He watched with envy every time a group assembled out of nowhere in some distant airport, train station, or park and danced to a familiar song from a throwback decade.

Chip stared at the words he wrote. He couldn't take them back. He looked around nervously. He didn't need to, but he did. He was in his house alone. Mrs. Clementine was out probably at Target, so it was just him and a massive dare he had just written to himself. He felt prodded and pushed in a good way.

This cannot be just any flash mob, he thought. It has to be local; it must involve dancing in public, and he needed to practice…a lot. He wasn't a natural dancer.

In his mind, which he knew could play tricks on him, his moves flowed like water. In reality, his arthritis could spike at the most inopportune time. His joints needed to warm up, especially on cold days.

He had just as much right as any other with a cancer diagnosis to chart a new course, a new journey. So, why not do a flash mob? He could think of four or five reasons why not and one big reason why he should.

His bucket list would be one for the ages and would begin and end at his local mall where any public spectacle would be welcomed by a town in need of a reboot.

His town, like so many others, was losing a war that threatened to eclipse towns like his through globalization. His town was on the wrong side of history and on an accelerating slide toward irrelevance.

There was one holdout – Chip's mall. That place was an anchor in his mundane life – a familiar place where he could reflect, meditate, find answers, and, of course, people watch.

Sitting in the food court on most weekends when he had no other pressing commitments, Chip enjoyed the detachment that came from being a spectator, an observer. In the food court, no one ever came up to him and asked for a report, really asked for anything. He was anonymous. It was refreshing.

On most Saturday mornings, you could find Chip positioned strategically at a corner table in the food court, with a beverage in hand, a most convenient excuse to watch human drama unfold before his eyes.

Sometimes, he would get splashed, sprayed, and even pushed. Having a front seat doesn't come without risk.

He hadn't seen it all, but he had seen much of all that was noble and empowering about the human spirit. He'd also seen life's darker, more intimate moments, most of which played out in or near the food court of a tiny mall in a tiny town in a tiny life.

He saw minor tiffs, a few squabbles, shoving, throw downs, walkaways, walkouts, and a few very public and very loud public brawls. There had been harmless pranks gone wrong, stopping people in their tracks.

Parents, seeing what others were fighting about, would forget where the children were, choosing to suppress their parental instincts for two more minutes to see who would win and how it would end.

Chip's bucket-list wish would take time and planning, but he needed to get going if this was going to happen by the December 22nd deadline, the last Saturday before Christmas Day – the flash mob performance day.

His first step weeks before the event was to sign up for an online audition to be in a flash mob. You couldn't just decide to participate in a flash mob, you had to be chosen which meant you had to interview.

This also meant you had to know the feature song for the flash-mob routine and practice your moves well in advance.

Following a few disjointed days of practice in his basement, he passed the audition and was given the thumbs up by three talking heads onscreen who called themselves judges.

After passing two rounds of online interviews, he was placed into a group and given rehearsal instructions and dates leading up to the big event. Chip was impressed with the organization; probably had some accountants in the mix, he thought.

They met together several times a week, diligently practicing their moves. In concept, their routine would be paired with another group's routine until all of these groups would be able to put on a really good flash mob at the appropriate time and place.

His 'crew' spanned all age groups. By day, they were accountants, police officers, social workers, retail employees, Uber drivers, and aspiring gamers. A real mix which gelled pretty quickly – they had to.

Their motivations were as different as their backgrounds. Chip was the token cancer guy – there was always one.

Bill – a police officer with twenty years on the force – was going through a midlife crisis and wasn't sure this was the right thing for him. Bill never participated in group sports and others had told him he needed a hobby.

Alexis, an army veteran turned guidance counselor, wanted to relive her last tour in Baghdad but on American soil. She thought a flash-mob experience might come close.

Mary, a long-time retail employee, was lonely and needed to connect and to feel again. A hardcore gamer, even she knew that her online persona had created a reputation at odds with how she wanted to finish out her sixties.

Anna was the youngest of them all. Enrolled in a nearby community college, she heard of an upcoming flash mob and signed up without question. She was also hoping to meet someone interesting and maybe a bit older than the guys she was used to dating.

Regina had been an Uber driver on weekends for the past year and used the extra cash to finance her regime of tanning sessions. She rarely talked and was always on her phone, texting away. She was the one everyone watched and wondered that if there was a mole in the group, it would be her. Despite these misgivings, people still told her their secrets.

Their practice times and locations were messaged no later than twenty-four hours out before the practice. If the group was compromised, they told each other; there would be no time for excuses.

A simple code word would be sent and they would disappear and then reappear again later.

Bill, the cop, struggled in practice. This was hard for him. Some of the moves were better preceded by a healthy stretch and warm-up, but he had stopped bending and squatting years ago when he was promoted to desk sergeant and life became easier.

Their practices lasted an hour. High-pitched commands from a team leader, who wouldn't be participating on 'game day,' barked at them incessantly like a Marine Corps drill instructor.

Those who struggled during practice had few options – get it right or get booted. Only one hadn't made the cut after a few routines.

No one was paid. Most did it for the publicity, not the fame or money. This would, however, be streamed live. Most thought about their next gig if this routine went truly viral. If they did well, there might by other invitations, more meaningful songs, and opportunities to rise up the flash mobber ranks.

Chip didn't know what to call himself within this group and hoped that 'flash mobber' was short-lived and replaced by something more empowering and less criminal sounding.

Sitting in the food court, Chip felt as ready as he was ever going to be. The practices had finished a couple of days ago. Now, he was in position, on the lookout, waiting for the cue.

There was nothing fancy about the cue. They had synchronized their watches.

The plan. At 12:45 p.m., fifteen minutes before Santa and his elves were scheduled to finish up and likely the time when parents and their kids had reached critical mass around the atrium area where the photos with Santa were being taken, a monotone voice over the intercom system would dryly thank everyone for coming to see Santa and that he would be leaving a few minutes early to load up his sleigh and begin his travels around the world. That was the plan.

Sure, there would be disappointment from the masses and Santa would be a little confused. Who wouldn't be? Santa hadn't planned to cut his shift fifteen minutes early. The elves would be okay. They did whatever Santa told them to do and none of them wore watches.

The theory went that he was paid by the hour and probably wouldn't mind getting off early if extra cash, say fifty bucks, from the flash-mob team was handed over to make things a little easier for him to go away – quietly and quickly. He would leave by the closest exit, elves in tow.

The elves might be confused at that point, but it wouldn't matter. The atrium would be cleared and there would be lots of parents and kids wondering what to do next.

The flash mob needed to perform when the crowds were at the biggest, and Santa and his elves had helped them get there. Thanks, Santa!

Time check. 12:40 p.m.

As he moved toward his designated spot, one they had practiced countless times before, he felt a kinship, even a connection with his fellow flash-mobbers. They'd been through so much together in such a short time.

The flash mob numbered about one hundred in all, broken down into several teams with team leaders. Not everyone was a dancer. Others preferred to be in a support role. Not everyone can dance and not everyone can support, so it just worked.

Support teams, with their special code names and polo shirts, were the one to clear the atrium area in short order when the first song started up over the P.A. system – that was their 'trigger.'

Clearing the atrium really meant politely asking Santa and his elves to vacate with the fifty bucks. They hoped the politely part would work. If not, they had the money at the ready to move things along faster with less wrangling or fuss if it came to it.

The one who ran everything, the flash-mob organizer, knew everyone can be bought for a price and had budgeted some petty cash to entice any recalcitrant Santa Claus to go somewhere else when the time came. He was right.

As planned, Claus took the money and the elves followed suit. Turns out, Claus was only getting minimum wage at that gig and he was near the end of his shift, so it was really a win-win all the way around.

Thus far, the flash-mob leader's plan was being executed perfectly. Santa was out of the way and a big crowd was looking for its next entertainment.

The music began. The flash mob slowly took form in the large atrium that functioned as an ice-skating rink during the summer months. Chip could see concerned looks from the shoppers as they saw the last glimpse of Santa and his elves as they went through the exit doors – Santa waved goodbye without looking back.

Some probably thought something was going to go down – most didn't. The clueless ones had budgeted their whole morning and past lunch to aimlessly wander around the mall so their senses were deadened and their kids were kept entertained.

But some did and pulled out their smartphones just in case. Those were the ones who tried to keep their kids quiet and from yanking on their arms with wild abandon, asking them for another donut or waffle cone as if they didn't have enough sugar in the body already.

Chip and his crew were stationed off to the right and, on cue, moved quickly to the center of the atrium. Chip knew they wouldn't be long in the center as they rotated in and out of the designated dance area, depending on their assignment, but it was nice to kick it off being on the first rotation.

Chip felt alive. His face was flushed, but it was more from the physical rigor of the warm-up exercises beforehand rather than the usual blushing and social anxiety.

Other crews looked flawless, he thought, looking around, watching them warm-up off to the side and away from onlookers as best as they could.

The beauty of a flash mob was that each crew worked in isolation so that secrecy was maintained until game day. Other teams were on the far side of the atrium. Chip wondered how it would all come together now that the day had finally arrived.

But that was for the flash-mob leader to figure out. Chip just had to perform his part, his role as practiced and believe and trust that it would all come together in one beautiful production and artistic expression. He had high hopes.

The music was loud, deafening, and a little scratchy. No one needed to speak – they had rehearsed this, mostly in silence. They were lost in their art form, their moves.

The routine was planned to run thirteen minutes, with a crescendo at the end with all of the dancers moving toward the crowd and each pulling a random stranger into the center of the atrium for a dance party.

If anyone resisted, they were to move onto the next person. If everyone resisted, then they were to grab a happy, smiling teenager with or without their parent's permission.

It was risky, but everything about the flash mob was risky. That's why Chip was there.

The first set in the routine wasn't the hardest but did come with its fair share of twists, turns, and unscripted lip sync from an overexcited flash mobber. Lip syncing was frowned upon, but what were they going to do now? It wasn't like they could hit the pause or rewind button. This was a live performance.

As Chip moved into position, he found himself in the soul of the collective – a conscious submission of will to the group psyche. He was part of something bigger than himself.

The music was pulsing, and he felt alive. He didn't think about cancer, his family-relationship issues, or what was for dinner. He looked around at those he practiced with over these past few weeks. Now he saw each of them in a new light. They were all his heroes. They had all come so far.

As he danced and looked into the crowd, he focused on the ones that weren't walking away, which was easy because this was the most exciting thing to happen to the town in recent memory. No one was leaving. They all had their reasons for staying, but it didn't matter. Flash mobs need large crowds, and they had one.

Chip knew the crowd wanted entertainment. For once, Chip thought, *I'm not a spectator. I'm a participant.* And that's when he saw three familiar faces a little way off, faces that belonged to three accountants that he worked with on the fourth-floor back in the office.

Technically, he mentored them. They were new hires and he had carefully coached them and tutored them in the serious study and practice of accounting procedures for the past three months as part of their onboarding requirements.

They didn't know Chip had a side other than serious, quiet, and methodical. They were about to be introduced to a side of Chip they never knew was possible.

They hadn't seen him yet, and it was only a matter of time when they would. His routine didn't allow him to gyrate in one place.

He would be making a full circle shortly, along with the others, careening around the outer area of the flash mob and toward them.

This was his mall, but he never considered that he might run into someone he knew from work. He had to stay professional, remain calm, and be true to his craft. But in mere seconds, he was on their side of the atrium and locked eyes with Brandon, the taller one in the group, and time slowed down.

As recognition set in, Chip could see Brandon mouthing words and pointing.

"It's Chip!" followed by, "Chip from Accounting, fourth-floor. He's one of us, guys!" It was a happy, shocked face. There was no disgust or recoil. There was acceptance, surprise, but acceptance.

Another in the group, Troy, dropped his funnel cake and didn't bother to look down, staring at Chip. This new world didn't make sense to him. Another, Nate, bent over and had some dry heaves.

Chip wasn't the type to blush unless things really went south. But when Brandon's and Chip's eyes locked, he felt the burn. The whole world was watching.

At work, many thought he was quite the stiff – a strait-laced, conservative's conservative. Certainly not the type of accountant that would dabble in the 'arts,' and certainly not participate in street-level entertainment.

This was a real shocker, Brandon thought. "Wow, just when you think you know someone," Brandon said, turning to Nate, only to find him sitting down on the ground, looking up to the ceiling with raised hands and forcing the air into his lungs.

All three were fixed and immovable from their spots, half-eaten funnel cakes in hand.

They didn't know. How could they? Chip was a showman at heart, an entertainer. There was a slice of extrovert in an otherwise iron-clad introvert frame with Chip. If there was a time to come out, it was now.

They were impressed. There he was, right in front of them. *He had some moves for sure. Not bad for an old guy*, they thought. Nate, still on the ground, was the only one that had not formed an opinion yet. He was still working through some breathing issues.

And then Chip and the rest of his team were in another part of the atrium, as other elements of the flash mob moved and performed.

It would be a while before his crew would make it to the front where his fellow accountants were, so he had a chance to catch his breath, but only once before he was off again.

He hadn't practiced the whole routine together in one run, only one part at a time. There wasn't enough time. There was.

Chip could only spend only so much time away from the house before she would catch on. So far, she hadn't. And so, he had assumed risk that everything would come together on game day.

But Chip was feeling his age and his thighs which were screaming at him. His heart was pounding. He thought this was the home stretch but wasn't sure. And that is when it happened.

His hamstrings cramped up – no sound, no pop, just shockwaves that went viral throughout his body, telling his mind to shut everything down and call for backup.

He couldn't fake it – the next routine would require everything he could muster, but there was nothing left to give. It was game over.

His crew noticed immediately and rallied around as best as they could, but you can improvise only so much before others start to wonder if what they were doing was intentional or just plain reactive.

He felt so helpless, so vulnerable, so dependent. From one embarrassing moment to another in less than a minute and on such a public stage. At some point, and he couldn't remember when, he let go of his colleague's hands and gravity took over.

He was swept up by much stronger flash mobbers from other crews as they quickly fashioned a way to save the routine from collapse.

Something had to give. The decision was made by someone who took charge with no official title, just an attitude and a desire to carry on no matter what.

Chip Clementine was carried to the center of the atrium. He was now the centerpiece of the act, a bright move since he was lying prostate and clearly in pain.

It was an amazing sight. As if paying homage to a fallen hero, the flash mobbers took turns dancing around (and through) Chip as he lay there dazed with hamstrings still aching.

He looked around and knew whatever was happening resonated with the crowd. He could read a room, or, in this case, the mall, and crowds now numbered in the hundreds, shoulder-to-shoulder, facing the atrium, spellbound, including the kids. Everyone was into it.

There were cheers, whoops, and those three accountants were chanting their college-fight song – they all attended the same one down south. Other people chanted in their own way. Some tried to mimic the flash-mob dance moves and got away with it.

Chip forgot he had cancer.

He forgot about the hamstrings. He felt the rush of a live performance – he felt accepted. As the last medley started to wind down and he could see in the flash mobbers' eyes that they had accomplished something that no one could take away from them, he was slowly lowered down from the makeshift human pyramid.

If he knew anything with confidence, it was that the medical stretcher provided by the local EMS crew was more comfortable than he would have guessed.

These first responders met him at the bottom of the pyramid with love in their eyes and Chip felt like he was in good hands. The paramedics were careful when they put him on the trolley and pushed him toward an exit, the closest one being down the other end of the mall.

Chip's departure route from the mall was lined with well-wishers and admirers. He and his new paramedic friends did the long walk, them with pride and Chip with embarrassment.

They paraded Chip through the crowds and along the shops and stands, sometimes twice. They were paramedics and no one had called in anything, so why not?

Chip didn't know where he was – there were so many people, but more than that he was strapped in and it wasn't as if he could direct traffic or sit up and figure out where he was going; they were in charge and they wore uniforms.

His anxiety started to meet up with the pulled hamstrings. He wasn't used to this much attention. Karaoke was different. There, on that stage, he was in charge. Here, they were. He hoped they knew where they going – they should, they're first responders, he said to himself.

Chip was an introvert's introvert, but he could play an extrovert quite well. In fact, most people thought Chip was a raving extrovert, but little did they know.

The only wrinkle in this theory was his onstage performances at the Irish pub every now and then when the mood for karaoke struck him, but that was easily explained.

Chip was indeed an introvert and many an introvert was in the entertainment business. Sure, he got nervous, but when he performed, he got a buzz that he couldn't find anywhere else.

Most other times, with each public interaction – at work, at the grocery store, etc., he consumed no small amounts of energy. At night, after a normal workday of interaction and conversation, he would collapse into bed and try to recharge his batteries before it all started again the next day.

Being the object of curiosity for the 15 minutes or so that it took for him to be paraded through the mall to the exit was draining, especially when someone tried to touch him.

Even though the paramedics doubled as security, they weren't the Israelis. Every once in a while, one or two hands got through and pinched and patted Chip.

Some of those hands belonged to Brandon, Troy, and Nate – three up and coming accountants who knew someone that could take a deep breath and jump right into a new world with new experiences without overthinking it.

Chip took it all in stride. Of course, it certainly didn't hurt when he got a particularly tight squeeze by a woman in the crowd, hoping for a connection with greatness.

Chapter 12
Chip Develops an 'Ism'

One of the more interesting things that came from Chip's foray into all thing's cancer was a discernible shift toward the extreme.

Cancer channeled Chip's propensities for cleanliness to new heights and new extremes. He'd always been a neat freak, but his cancer diagnosis gave him a license to explore, to let his idiosyncrasies run wild and for his nuances to be more nuanced.

Since the diagnosis, but especially after the holidays, Chip had become quickly attracted to minimalism, finding ways to simplify his life – all aspects of his life.

He attempted a measure of this at home in early January by conducting a systematic review of each room in the house, starting with one of the guest bedrooms. Bedrooms were easy targets.

Christmas decorations were stacked vertically in closets at the expense of hangers and clothes. Shoe boxes wouldn't stand a chance and would be sent packing despite their objections.

This would be an easy sell to Mrs. Clementine, he thought.

In Chip's long marriage, if there was one thing he had learned over the years, it was to make sure he got the green light from his better half before doing any room makeovers.

His singular challenge, whether it was room makeovers or anything else that involved potential downsizing, was convincing Mrs. Clementine of the need to do so. Easier said than done.

Mrs. Clementine was a hoarder of epic proportions and found giving anything away as abhorrent. She was most definitely anti-minimalism and most emphatically pro-maximumism, if that was even a word.

Rarely emotional, she became a possessed spirit at the mention of words such as simplify, downsize, or reduce. Each of her precious possessions, experiences, trips, events, parties, and any other physical objects had earned the right to live in a particular room for the rest of their natural lives.

Things had feelings, personalities, and rights – just like people.

She walked into the guest bedroom as Chip sized up the contents in the closet for potential clearing. The recommended approach was all over the internet and popularized through some cable T.V. shows – keep, give away, or throw away. But he hadn't practiced his pitch and it showed.

Everyone was doing it, Chip tried to say with confidence. He tripped over his words and they both knew what would come next. She would say and he would do.

All it took was a few words, really just one, for Mrs. Clementine to set Chip straight. Chip knew which way his bread was buttered. The answer was no – short and sweet.

Chip went back to the living room and slumped down on the couch. He made mental notes to not call his three daughters and ask them to come and collect their high-school yearbooks and half-filled journals. There would be no calling and no collecting.

The yearbooks and journals would stay right where Mrs. Clementine had put them. They were trapped just like Chip was.

Chip held other grandiose ideas about transforming (code for downsizing) his home but had to get his plan through Mrs. Clementine, and it had been quashed before it had a chance to breathe. So, he tried one more time and threw down the cancer card. Maybe that would work.

Mrs. Clementine saw the hurt on Chip's face and was surprised that he'd come back with a rebuttal. He never did that.

After a few minutes of hearing him out some more, she decided to give him a little, not much, but a little. He did have cancer, although she thought he was embellishing like he always did when he came back from seeing Doctor Raj.

She would relent on the subject, she told him…but just this once. Two thoughts came into her mind.

The first thought was that more than likely Chip really did have cancer, however minor it probably was, and probably needed some project to make him feel good about himself.

The second thought was that the garage was a mess – Chip's mess. Her stuff in other rooms could never be called a mess, but Chip's stuff could be. *We haven't parked the cars there since Lindsay left the house*, she thought.

Anything in that place would be an improvement, she reasoned with herself, since all the important stuff she kept track of had to be in a climate-controlled environment. It was settled. The garage would be the compromise.

He could simplify the garage and only the garage, she told him flatly.

That little project took several days and gave him a nice lift. Chip was past his prime in more than ways than one but found a new level of energy in moving boxes, going to the dump, and even making a few sales with the neighbors on some of the gear he had in there.

He moved some things around, got rid of even more, and stayed on task, foregoing his favorite T.V. shows and the evening news. He had the license to create space in the back and organize his tools, even his workbench.

The garage, without a doubt, was a nice-sized project, taking a weekend-and-a-half. When he was done, he knew his crusade wasn't over. He thought about where else he could apply his talent and passion. The rest of the house was *verboten.* There was only one other logical outlet for his 'ism' – work, specifically his fourth-floor.

He could think of no better place to simplify on the fourth-floor than the main breakroom – a real mess!

The breakroom was a planned open space at the western corner of the fourth-floor. It served many functions, not the least of which was to offer caffeinated drinks to weary accountants and other staff who wanted to be accountants.

Chip had chosen not to announce his intention to clean things up there ahead of time and, instead, shown up on Monday with a trolley filled to capacity with household-cleaning products and determination.

He procured some yellow crime-scene tape and decided that only by sealing off the breakroom area would he be able to work his magic.

The yellow tape commanded attention. In the breakroom, he took everything out of the cupboards and threw half of it away, including cups, cutlery, and dish towels.

His thinking was clear – scarcity begets order rather than panic. Chip reasoned when people see less of something, they will respect the place more.

His vision for the breakroom was a place where people moved effortlessly with fewer cups, spoons, and napkins. It followed that ever thereafter, such a workplace transformation, others would be pleasant, polite, and respectful to each other.

Chip installed a couple of webcams in the breakroom, positioned to capture people's kindnesses and considerations and, of course, the transgressions.

He would capture those moments when they would all be on their best behavior, hopefully. Then, he would play back those moments in monthly training. It would be great.

He was especially focused, however, on curbing the darker side of human nature in others, feeling responsible for the enforcement of this newly created surveillance state.

So, he went to work in the breakroom.

The whole thing took about an hour. When the breakroom was 'simplified,' Chip took down the crime-scene tape and declared the breakroom open for business.

Each expressed amazement with the changes. The microwave was sparkling clean, the sink spotless. There was less clutter, but soon people started to wonder where 'their' mug was which always held such a prominent place near the cookie jars.

Come to think of it, many realized that the cookie jars were gone. Where are the coconut cookies? The vibe changed and Chip felt a slight heat working its way up his neck and onto his face. The accusations grew louder and the room no longer felt warm and friendly.

Chip attempted to explain the wonderful improvements to the breakroom, but it was too late. A mob was forming.

Chip had become the target for their pent-up anger. Making this worse for Chip was that he picked a Monday to launch his creative concept. No one is receptive to good ideas on Mondays, try Tuesdays, Chip.

People are grumpy on Mondays, especially on January Mondays. The junior staff was especially grumpy on Mondays as they had to recommit to a life that didn't jive with their school's promotional brochures when they considered accounting as a possible career. In those brochures, accountants smiled and worked together for a bright corporate future.

Chip hadn't seen his co-workers this upset in a while. He saw emotions that day that would have been surprising, even on the third floor with the wild ones in Marketing, who were known to show emotion and overdramatize their arguments.

He knew he lost his battle when later that morning, someone exploded an unopened macaroni-and-cheese packet in the microwave deliberately, told everyone about it, and pranced off in a righteous huff.

Management hadn't intervened throughout all of this for one good reason – they enjoyed watching the train wreck. They'd read enough case studies in business school to know how this would play out; they just hadn't the chance to observe something like this 'in the field.'

Many of them hung around long after the dumping of the sugar on the floor and a few anti-Chip epitaphs were written on one of the cupboard doors. For once, they were not the object of scorn. Chip was taking the heat and he was one of them – even better, they said to themselves in their special breakroom.

They would snicker and gloat. What a cover we have in Chip, they said as they huddled together near a receptionist they could trust.

Chip's idealism didn't die that day, but it did take a few hits to the groin. After scaling back at his house and relegated to the garage and then meeting with such resistance in the breakroom, he could only take solace in his cubicle.

His cubicle, however, was already oversimplified on account of him being, well, Chip. So, in an act of defiance to all authority figures in his, he sharpened all his pencils and emptied his trash.

It had been a while.

Chapter 13

Drawing Strength from
the Past and the Present

Looking at Chip, one might think he spent his working days tethered to a desk with a calculator in one hand and colored pencils in another. One would be mostly right.

However, Chip hadn't always lived and breathed numbers. Sure, he looked the part, don't they all – starched white shirts, conservative ties, and the ever-present lapel pin. But Chip's past was anything but orderly, synchronized, and planned.

Before the accounting trade, Chip lived life on the edge, taking one day at a time and without a planner. Every day was a dice roll. He relied on his wits, a full head of hair, and a fake British accent.

When asked about his past, he was vague. He liked to keep things buried deep. When he answered, there was a faint, wistful smile from a man that had been what few could have imagined and where even fewer could have lived.

His fourth-floor colleagues of today wouldn't have recognized the Chip of yesterday. Only his closest friends – not the ones at work; the ones that he traveled with to conventions and conferences knew his past.

They knew what he carried with him every day – regret and longing – wistful memories of a time when the spray of saltwater, the feel of a crisp anorak, and the feel of a taut line on a fishing trawler came back when he least expected it to taunt him time and time again.

Yes, Chip had been an Alaskan fisherman!

It felt good to say it out loud, Chip thought. At his core, he was a man from the sea with a few years under his belt in his younger years working the commercial fishing routes in the Bering Sea.

Back then, he was about as far from being an accountant as one could imagine. Alaska fisherman didn't have calculators and hadn't the time to do math – they were fishing the big game. Tallying numbers was for other folk.

As a self-proclaimed fisherman, Chip had wrestled with the fury of the seas and had the wooly, itchy cap to prove it, sort of.

Technically, he wasn't an Alaskan fisherman as you would see on the documentary shows. He was a deckhand and not a deckhand on the boat per se.

He did all the things that a deckhand did on a boat; he just did it onshore, in the harbor, when the boats came back in after…well…fishing.

He could claim he was a fisherman since he was connected by payroll to a shipping company. And he did like to be around ships.

He just had a medical condition, more of a mental than physical one really, which challenged his comfort level with seawater. So, he was a fisherman in the most loosest of terms and connections and most people wouldn't know the difference, anyway, back east when he visited his family.

Chip loved the ocean, loved being near it, just not on it – made him queasy. He did the best thing he could at the time and supported the fishery business by being the best land-based deckhand he could be.

Real Alaska fisherman appreciated what Chip did for them. Not everything can look at themselves in the mirror, claim they're a fisherman, and then never set foot on a boat.

He was honorarily listed on the payroll as deckhand. He would take that any day of the week.

In truth, the closest Chip got to tapping into the spirit and comradery of his fellow fishermen was when he waved them off each time they left for a fishing trip.

As the ships faded from view, he returned dutifully to clean out the stalls and walkways, knowing that he was an integral part of an elite group that risked their lives to bring salmon and king crab to America's dinner tables.

Saying goodbye was never easy each time they left, but he knew they might be back in a week or three and Chip would be there to help offload the bounty. When they did leave, he would make the long walk back up the hill to the hostel and read books about deep-sea fishing.

There was no television, so Chip just read and penned a few lines of poetry every so often about the perils of tuna fishing off the Alaskan coast.

Chip had a pretty good imagination but still took notes when the actual fisherman would tell him stories. He lived his life through them more times than he'd care to admit.

He would think about those times, and when he did, he would occasionally look behind his computer monitor to admire his small Alaskan fishing-trawler replica right next to his pencil sharpener.

The inscription on below the boat was in italics which gave it a rustic look.

To Chip!
The best Deckhand on the South End of Kodiak's North Harbor.
Fair Winds and Following Seas!

Chip took pride in how compartmentalized his life and how far he'd come since Alaska when transactions were handled in cash or bartered in foodstuffs.

There were those who would never know his past and that was okay…for now. If there was anything that Chip brought forward from that life to this one, it was the mantras that he said to himself regularly to steel him for the day's events. Sure, it wasn't Alaska anymore with its three hours of daylight, but some days at the office got really tough and saying certain things to himself actually made him feel like a better person.

Some would call what he did mindfulness, repeating positive messages at the start of each morning before his first of many cups of high-octane coffee. Chip just called it self-talk.

Daily mantras were another staple in Chip's routine that helped him manage stress and anxiety, but mostly anxiety.

There weren't many lines in his daily mantra, but they got him moving in the right direction, especially with the current struggles he was going through that started with 'C' and ended with 'ancer.'

His first mantra grounded him when things started to go off the rails, and it was a nod to his love for science fiction which, to him, was not fiction at all – it was just a reality that humanity had not yet discovered.

Mantra #1: *Everything about Star Wars is real – the Jedi Knights, lightsabers, Stormtroopers, Darth Vader – everything is completely real. Star Trek, on the other hand, is completely made up and the product of someone's imagination.*

As a Jedi Knight, I can be a force for good in the universe and especially here in my cubicle. While others may laugh at the lightsaber I bought online, they secretly wish they had one in the event of a disturbance in the force.

Mantra #2: *Just because people throw things at me for no apparent reason doesn't mean they don't like me. It means they need my help and are just trying to get my attention to request my assistance because I am in demand.*

When people are desperate for help, they don't care whether it's a crumpled piece of paper or a partially filled hot coffee cup – they need help and they need it now. I'm known as a fixer and it feels good to be wanted.

Mantra #3: *I have stayed in my current position for a disproportionate time compared to my peers because management has surmised that I'm the only one capable of training others in this field, especially those new to the English language.*

I know I'm sought after, but it's not something I brag about. Some of us are indispensable and management has pegged me as one. With great power comes responsibility.

Mantra #4: *Most people say the opposite of how they feel about me for any number of reasons. I won't judge them. I can empathize with those that appear to be frustrated or even confrontational with me. I appreciate all of them and feel part of the team.*

***

Mantras were a staple of Chip's daily routine, but so were random events designed to test his wits and his endurance.

Being challenged to a contest against a worthy opponent kept him on his toes, and there was no worthier opponent for this particular game he would play than Mike from Sales. It was harmless fun really, but it kept Chip sharp. He never knew when he would be challenged.

Their contest was a stare down contest, a contest to see which one would blink first, succumbing to the pressure and foregoing their place of glory for the day. For this type of contest, there was no need for prep time – just healthily alert eyelids.

These unannounced competitions kept Chip on his toes. *It could get scary, especially when Mike would jump out from a broom closet or another and initiate the contest of wills. But scary can be good,* Chip thought.

The time and place were never announced. That would be too predictable, giving either of them enough time to prepare.

Chip didn't want to be prepared. He was prepared in every other aspect of his life and these epic showdowns was a temporary escape clause in his contract with himself to live a little, if only for a few minutes at a time.

The prize for winning never varied also – one chocolate-covered, custard-filled donut delivered to the victor's cubicle without fuss – just a nod of the head and a mutual understanding that in this jungle, you were either the lion or the gazelle.

Chip and Mike from had been locked in this mortal conflict for years. On some days, it was the only thing for which they looked forward.

They never kept score, but Chip was pretty sure he was ahead, counting his victories through hand-carved notches on his wooden chair. Chip knew it was pride talking, but he'd finally found something where he could compete at the highest level.

When eyes locked and the lights dimmed, voices were hushed and time seemed to move like a dream.

There was nothing weird, strange, or perverse between them – just two men having a bit of sport and exercising their competitive nature when the moment presented itself.

The longest they'd gone before the first one blinked was three minutes and four seconds.

Chip won that one but only because he practiced keeping his eyes open the night before watching repeated car-chase scenes on a retro 70s T.V. channel.

Chip tried to build muscle memory into his eyelids by propping them open with toothpicks for extended periods of time as a way to practice for his showdowns. Occasionally, that brilliant idea would backfire and he would find himself in the ER along with others trying to reclaim their lost youth.

Today could be the day though – he would be ready; he was born ready. To the victor go the spoils.

***

And then he smelled something, something that distracted him more than the thought of a possible showdown with Mike. Burned popcorn. Chip's blood start to simmer toward a slow boil.

As a hunter, he could smell, see, hear, and feel things before others could. It was a gift he found hard to explain to others without coming across as elevated.

The smell of burned popcorn was a clear no-no on the floor according to his own set of rules of conduct. One such self-declared rule was no burnt popcorn in the microwave – ever.

Call it a pet peeve, call it a mortal sin, but there had to be checks and balances and someone had to pay for disobedience. Burnt popcorn punctured his karma and put his universe in spin mode. Only he could put the genie back in the bottle.

The usual reason for such a *faux-pas* was that someone had cooked the popcorn for too long. He hadn't found any other reason yet.

He had an idea which breakroom was the scene of mishap – *such a rookie move*, Chip thought, as he followed his nose out the door and down the hallway toward the breakroom.

If he ran fast enough, he might be able to catch the culprit. *Some people lack common manners*, he thought.

He continued his mental rant. All you have to do is press '1' on the keypad, he thought, which actually says the word popcorn next to it.

How can anyone fail with such a simple task?

There his rant was over, but he couldn't help but think about the number of times he had briefed it to breakroom crowds over the years – no one listened, no one cared until it was too late.

He found her in the breakroom next to the microwave, clearly unhinged – Emma!

The culprit could have been any man or woman but Emma. He had such a high opinion of her on account of her tastes in Indian food. But she had burnt the popcorn and had to go on his special list. Chip's inner circle was getting smaller and smaller.

It was increasingly clear who could be trusted and who wasn't going to get invited to his Lord of the Rings weekend movie marathon this weekend.

The morning continued but not without more drama.

When the fire alarm went off, Chip was halfway through comparing Disney cruises. He'd narrowed it down to three candidates and had ignored emails all morning.

The fire alarm was incredibly loud. His eyes broke contact with the screen. Chip had only one choice.

He would drop and roll underneath his cubicle without fanfare or public announcement. When everyone was gone, he would complete the cruise-line booking.

The website told him he had only nine minutes and fifty-nine seconds to book and so, like everything in his life, he trusted 'them' completely.

The hardest part of those first few seconds between the fire alarm and coming up with his drop-roll-and-book strategy was having to lie next to Sally, his cubicle office neighbor to his back and right.

She followed the office drill to a tee and was now staring at Chip under the desks with fear in her eyes. Sally needed assurance. Chip had none. He was thinking about ocean views, cabin upgrades, and a possible cancer discount if they were inclined to give it.

As quickly as it started, the drill was over. Management sent the email out saying how everyone had done such a great job following procedures. Now, settling back into his chair, Chip noticed an old calendar under a stack of papers he never disturbed.

I must have banged the desk when I dropped to the floor, Chip thought.

There, near the bottom of the stack, he saw an old calendar with a big red 'X' on the day that changed everything.

When they changed out the copier machines in favor of ones that were actually copiers and printers, Chip thought he'd lost his mind. All sense of normal went out the door when these new copiers showed up one dreary, cold Monday in November a year ago.

His copier had been faithful for the last ten years and had waited on him like an old friend. His copier obeyed every instruction and treated him as a real person. Chip felt more connected and alive each and every time he scanned or copied from this faithful friend.

And so, every 7th of November, Chip planned a variety of anniversary tributes to his old copier. He'd enlisted others in the day's somber anniversary – it hadn't been hard.

There had been all too many others ready to share their own stories, their own heartbreaking losses.

Over some candles and popcorn in the breakroom but mostly where the copier used to be, they would recount their interactions with the one thing that had given them solace in their own personal struggles.

Some were more open than others. Some required a hug, a few required medical attention, and one triggered a call to security out of an abundance of caution.

Chip, as the organizer, had a special place in their hearts, though, for keeping the spirit alive and for remembering the good times.

They say closure is necessary to move on, but Chip disagreed with the professionals on the subject of grieving.

Chip knew the hearts of those present as they gathered with their candles, singing their chants, loud enough for management to hear. Management would listen, surely.

Bring back our copier, Mr. Jarvis!

Chapter 14

Take Your Dog to Work Day

If there was a corporate event Chip didn't embrace fully, it was the annual Take Your Dog to Work Day. Most people just called it 'Doggie Day.'

But Chip's fight with cancer was about to give him access to new possibilities and open him up to opportunities previously closed to him by virtue of being, in this case, pet-less.

Doggie Day was a few weeks after Valentine's Day, when the weather was still cold, and people couldn't imagine what warmer days were like. So, management, in their infinite wisdom, decided that those with pet dogs could bring them in and the whole office would get a collective morale lift, or at least that was the theory.

The event was specific – showing off your dogs to the world. He didn't begrudge anyone their opportunity to 'present' their canines to their co-workers but still had some mixed feelings over the subject. Cats were exempt, for example.

Each year, the event followed the same script. His colleagues paraded their dogs around the office like trophies and then were invited to walk down a makeshift model runway to be recognized and applauded for the special relationship they had with each other.

Chip always pined after a dog. Mrs. Clementine hadn't allowed it, and he wasn't allowed to bring it up in conversation. So, he kept his feelings in check.

It was tough, though, to keep a straight face when then they visited his parents' house and shared the dinner table with Mom and Dad's twin Chihuahuas.

Those twins had their own chairs, their own plates. They sat eye-level with everyone because of the raised, special cushions they had, strapped down on the chairs to ensure there would be no accidents. Chip's parents believed that dogs are people too.

Chip loved dogs and he lived vicariously through others who had dogs. He wasn't a snob – he loved all breeds, especially when colleagues would sneak their dogs into the office on a casual Friday. Chip would look the other way and sometimes create a distraction if management was nearby.

Today was a special day – Doggie Day. The event had sponsorship, money, some trinkets, and, of course, a makeshift 'model' runway.

Ms. Spencer (everyone called her 'Leslie') had organized this event every year for the past ten years. She planned each of these events down to the smallest details and it showed.

She owned a Labradoodle which was not technically correct since the father was a poodle and the mother was a Labradoodle. So, her dog was really a Labradoodle poodle, but that was splitting hairs. Chip tried to correct her once but walked it back when he saw how defensive she was about the Labradoodle breed.

When the big day arrived, dogs and their owners had free reign on the fourth-floor, actually on all floors. They pretty much did whatever they wanted and the humans followed them around.

The hallmark of the event was the dog parade.

At a certain time in the morning, right before the catered lunch, Leslie announced each dog's name from preformatted paper that the owner was required to fill out, including how to enunciate the dog's name correctly. With Leslie, everything had to be just right.

Each owner chose the song they wanted to play in the background as both owner and dog would strut their stuff down the runway. Some owners did less strutting and more cajoling/pulling on the leash to get their dogs moving.

After the runway walk, owner and dog were interviewed by Leslie.

"How long have you both been 'together'?"

"What's your dog's favorite snack?"

"When was the moment when you knew your companion was something special?"

There were other questions along the same line. You get the point. It was a love fest.

Most said their moment was when they picked their pup out of a litter at someone's house or in a pet store. Others took more time going off-topic and savoring the spotlight.

In the days leading up to the event, Chip thought he might have a case to petition Mrs. Clementine for a dog. He did have breast cancer after all, and there was this event coming up. If there was any time to ask for a dog, it had to be now.

One evening, Chip cooked a particularly good spinach gnocchi with meatballs for obvious and not so obvious reasons.

"So, how did you like the gnocchi?" Chip asked his wife.

He tried to ask innocently but wasn't sure how it came across. *Let's start with this and see how it goes*, Chip thought. Monday was Italian night and he always did the gnocchi.

"It's okay…a little light on the garlic. Why do you ask? What are you up to?" She was getting suspicious. "What do you mean?" He knew she could see through him.

"I think you know what I mean. Is it happening soon?" she asked pointedly.

Dang it! Chip thought.

How did she know the Take Your Dog to Work Day was coming up? *I didn't see it on her calendar on the fridge, and she puts everything on that calendar. Maybe she went digital with her calendar? That would explain it*, Chip thought, still confused and needing closure.

Mrs. Clementine knew this conversation was going to come up. It always came up this time of year. She thought his attempt to soften her up with a discussion about the gnocchi was unusually clever.

Typically, Chip went straight in with a request, to his peril. He had tried this before.

"Yes, it's next week. (Slight pause.) Darling, it's so painful to watch. You know how much I love dogs," Chip said.

"Chip, we've talked about this. No dogs, ever."

She was resolute. Her name should have been Mrs. Resolute, not Mrs. Clementine. That would have done her more justice.

"Come on, Mrs. C."

He called her that sometimes because he felt that she felt a little elevated when addressed formally.

"You know this time it's different."

"Different?" *Where's he going with this?* she thought.

"I have cancer." (Another pause for dramatic effect.) "I need this, I really do."

If there was a moment, this was the moment. There was a long pause before she answered back. There had never been this long a pause before on this subject, and they had this conversation every year about the same time. Maybe this time was different.

"Maybe we can work something else," she said casually.

"Sure," he tried to act cool, but his pulse was quickening, and he was a little out of breath.

"You can have a..." Chip was on the edge of his couch, almost falling forward.

"You can have... (she said it twice when she really wanted him to understand what she was saying) a pet tortoise."

Chip slumped back into the couch like he had been mortally wounded.

"A tortoise!" he said dejectedly. *What's a tortoise? Is that the same thing as a turtle?* Chip wondered. Mrs. C, ignoring his dramatics, continued. "But you are responsible for everything, Chip. I mean it. You clean up after it. You take it for walks, etc."

She had to give him something, and the 'etc.' thrown in was deliberate. A tortoise in her mind was the perfect compromise. Chip would have his pet, she had reasoned quickly, a pet that would be orders of magnitude easier to deal with, to live with than a dog.

Chip's 'pet' would be something that takes a week to walk from one end of the kitchen to the other, not running around from one room to the other, making a lot of commotion.

How easy would it be for this tortoise to meet with foul play before it really started to get on her nerves? she thought and smiled a little.

Chip was looking at her, thinking of what to say next but couldn't find the words. She had him.

Also, she thought, tortoises hibernate for a good chunk of the year. It will be tucked away nicely in their glass cage, sleeping their days away. Yes, she thought, this would get him off my back about having a dog. This might work out very nicely.

Chip was thinking carefully before responding to his wife's first-ever relenting of him getting a pet in the home.

151

Did she know that no one takes a tortoise out for a walk? Dogs, yes, tortoises, no – not even close. What does that even look like? he thought.

He must be careful about what he said next. He had blown tentative agreements with Mrs. Clementine time after time and could not afford to blow it on this one.

Okay, here we go, Chip thought.

"A tortoise. Thanks, darling. You won't regret this." He got up from the couch and backed away slowly. This was a breakthrough. There would be time for further concessions later, but not now.

Chip patted himself on the back subconsciously for saying the right things, avoiding the usual gaffs that got him into trouble. He still felt cheated.

Tortoises are not dogs. She couldn't have picked a more passive creature in the animal kingdom.

Tortoises took whatever you gave them, and they gave nothing back. And taking 'Horace' for a walk, is she kidding? There would be no walking, just staring. Chip staring at Horace and Horace staring at Chip. Both waiting for the other to initiate movement. Well, good luck if you're counting on Horace to get you moving. It won't happen.

So, for the first time in their marriage, Chip went to the pet shop and bought a pet, not a cuddly toy.

He walked confidently to the reptile section, past the cats and dogs in their small cubby holes. It was like they were saying to him, "Chip, a tortoise, really?" He didn't care.

At the back of the store, he found the tortoise section.

There were three tortoises in the cage, but none of them moved. They didn't blink when Chip pressed his face against the glass to get a better look.

That's when he remembered they were tortoises, not dogs, and tortoises don't move unless the world is coming to an end and no one is going to take care of them anymore.

I am sure, he thought, the tortoises would find a way to put one foot in front of another. Maybe it was all really an act on the part of the tortoises and they actually did move like other four-legged animals but just kept a really good secret about their mobility.

Chip was slightly giddy with excitement. One of them would be his and soon.

The pet-shop assistant appeared with a big smile and a mop of hair. To Chip, Brycen looked eternally optimistic and full of life. But Brycen was a college dropout, working in a pet store to support his online gaming addiction.

His smile was real but only because he knew he got paid later, and paydays were always an excuse to meet up with his gamer friends and spend that night and the next gaming it up and delaying personal hygiene.

Brycen, to his credit, was helpful. Chip asked a volley of questions about each of the tortoises, their species, dietary habits, sleeping times.

When he asked about sleeping times, Brycen gave Chip an odd look and told him that the tortoises sleep all day, except for a brief time when they eat lettuce, but that only lasted about five minutes.

"The only thing they do fast is eat and poop," said Brycen, preferring not to judge Chip's tastes in pets. *He clearly wants a dog*, Brycen thought.

"My wife says they hibernate for half the year. Is that true?" Chip asked.

He couldn't believe anything hibernated, let alone for months. Chip wanted this to end soon so he could choose his 'Horace' and get back to the house where he could set up the glass cage.

Brycen continued, "Well, that is true for most of the tortoises, but this particular one (he pointed to the future Horace) is a Mediterranean red-footed tortoise who doesn't hibernate. He's active all year."

Brycen kept smiling with a smile that begged further questioning. But Brycen was faking it. He wasn't sure what he was talking about, since he started work there yesterday, coming off of another short-term gig in retail that had not worked out so well for him either.

He was desperate to be seen as credible, especially during his first week of work. Brycen's sole qualification for this minimum wage job was he knew the difference between a rabbit and a guinea pig with just two prompts from the manager.

"Are you sure?" Chip saw the hesitation in Brycen.

"Absolutely," Brycen spoke with so much confidence. Chip wished he had this much confidence when he explained the company's financials to non-accountants.

Chip used to be a confident person, but the consistent second-guessing by others in brightly lit conference rooms over the years had worn him down.

He felt under the microscope every time he entered a room with fluorescent lighting. He took heart from his friends at work, who tried to dim the lights when they knew Chip would be in their meeting. Chip wondered when and where he would get his confidence back, if ever.

A cancer diagnosis had shaken him to the core and, maybe, Horace the tortoise was what was needed to get Chip back to a more confident place. Maybe Horace could be the catalyst to give him his mojo back in a way that only a tortoise could.

He took Horace home. Horace rode in the front seat – no seatbelt.

Mrs. Clementine met them both at the front door. There was going to be a new member of the household. Horace's custom-designed room was a glass cage in the kitchen and it was prominently placed in the farthest, most remote part of the kitchen, next to the food pantry which was next to the door that led conveniently to the garage.

Mrs. Clementine laid down the rules for Chip. She spouted out the rules like one barks out military orders.

Horace could walk the kitchen floor once a day after his meal, unrestrained and unsupervised. The standard would be time, not distance.

If Horace was able to make his walk within 30 minutes, all well and good. If not, he would be picked up wherever he was at and put back in the cage. Mrs. C. was not going to spend her afternoon seeing if Horace could walk the entire kitchen floor.

She had other things to do with her life than watch Horace, like her nails or daytime soaps. That was the agreement, but it had come at a price for Chip.

When Horace arrived, those first few days had been harder than imagined for Mrs. Clementine. She couldn't get used to seeing Horace staring up at her while she did dishes or while she switched channels between her favorite soap channels.

Within a week, thanks to Horace, Mrs. Clementine had developed a minor eye twitch. It was barely noticeable. She would see it out every time she was near a mirror. She wondered if others could tell she had an eye twitch. They could.

The Take Your Dog to Work Day event came quickly. Chip and Horace were not prepared for Horace's debut, but is one ever prepared for a debut?

Chip made sure his version of a dog, Horace, would be one of the first to be introduced as he paraded/held him down the makeshift model runway on the fourth-floor.

Chip's angle for Horace's participation was that this is really a Take Your Pet, rather than a Dog, to Work Today and should not be confined to dogs.

He got pre-approval from Leslie surprisingly easy to parade Horace even though he was not a dog. Leslie, a fan of animal rights, saw no reason why Chip and Horace couldn't join the fun, and with a one-sentence email, she approved a new category of entrant in this year's grand affair. This year, dogs and tortoises. Next year? Who knows!

Leslie barked instructions over the handheld microphone, getting everyone and everything ready for the runway. The line curved around the floor and down the fire-escape stairs. The dogs were a motley crew of assorted colors, sizes, and sentiment. Some didn't want to be there.

For most of the dogs, this was a new adventure, a big leap from being locked in their homes all day while both of their human parents were out earning their dual incomes.

For others, it was a chance to mark their territory and climb a few social ladders.

When Leslie introduced Franklin, chocolaty-golden noodle as the first dog to be paraded, Franklin urinated spontaneously at the start of the runway. Maybe it was nerves, maybe it wasn't.

Franklin didn't have inhibitions as humans do and sprayed, as he walked, down the runway to the amazement of the crowds. If Franklin knew anything, he knew that owning real estate is nine-tenths of the law and marking his territory was possession in his world.

The onlookers were conflicted. Most wanted to support the event, but some, especially those up close to the catwalk, didn't want to get caught in Franklin's spray.

A few made a bolt for the exit, but others were too tightly packed in their seats and had to grin and bear it.

Leslie's appeal for calm was admirable but didn't have its desired effect. Franklin in his territory-marking mode had careened off the catwalk and directed his 'attention' toward the podium. Leslie's dress was collateral damage in Franklin's wild abandon.

This was the first time Leslie had been up close and personal with other dogs with such different manners. Her dog never did anything wrong or step out of line. Her dog knew exactly where the line was.

Her voice over the microphone wavered, made worse by the static, and reduced her commands to barely a whisper.

An emotionally spent and physically disheveled Leslie with a soiled dress did her best to get the event moving again. She welcomed everybody and asked the second dog owner and dog to begin their walk down the runway.

There were twenty or so of Chip's colleagues that brought their dogs to the event. Chip and Horace were number three in the lineup.

Leslie wasn't sure how a tortoise would be received, so she put Horace closer to the top of the lineup. People would look past most things in the early rounds of judging, or so she thought.

Leslie mitigated the concern about having a non-dog in the dog event by announcing that today was about pets and emphasized that pets come in all shapes and sizes. Chip never felt more included and silently thanked Leslie for those kind words. Horace couldn't have cared less. He was fixated on an apple near a window.

When it was Chip's turn to walk with Horace, he did so without regrets. Chip was the only one without a leash…and a dog. Nothing bothered Horace. Chip thought Horace had nerves of steel.

Horace's composure only reinforced Chip's conviction that he and Horace were meant for each other. Maybe, matches were made in Heaven.

In the few short days Chip was with Horace, he was impressed by Horace's quiet, chill vibe. More than once, Chip had prodded Horace in the soft underbelly to see if he was awake, conscious, or both. Horace usually responded with a characteristic slight nod of the head as if to say, "It's all good, Brother!"

When Chip stepped onto the runway and into the bright lights, Horace was right there with him, looking dead ahead.

There was a certain pace each person had to keep in order for this thing to end within the hour. Nonetheless, they walked with pride down the runway and toward the dessert table where Leslie had repositioned the podium after the earlier fiasco with Franklin.

Chip wanted this moment to last a little longer. Mid-way down the runway, he stopped and decided that he needed to make a statement about how this event could grow to encompass other household pets. He was the voice of a silent generation and knew they would give him license to speak on their behalf.

During this impromptu speech, Chip had placed Horace carefully down on the runway. The spectators gave their 'oohs' and 'ahhs' as they saw Horace on all fours, standing proud.

What Chip hadn't predicted, however, was that all the dogs lined up behind Chip had been watching Horace with fascination, enough so that when Horace was 'unprotected,' they had launched collectively into a sprint, breaking free of their owners' leashes to zero in on poor Horace.

Surrounded and separated from Chip, Horace endured sniffing, pushing, and prodding. The dogs had never encountered a tortoise with his hard outer shell and his no blinking.

Horace, feeling threatened, went to his own happy place. With his head firmly tucked into his body, Horace became, for all intents and purposes, a soccer ball.

A few of the larger Danes attempted to pull Horace out of his shell but, in the physical push and pull of it all, launched Horace from one end of the runway to the other, like a Ping-Pong ball batted in one direction to the next.

The spectacle of a tortoise shell sliding would have been funny if it didn't pose such a danger for poor Horace. Who would have thought such fun-loving dogs would be so vindictive?

The only way out of this and quickly was for someone in authority to bring order to chaos. Leslie knew that this was her cue, despite feeling that this would be the last Take Your Dog to Work Day ever on her watch.

Leslie called for order, asking everyone to retrieve their dogs, especially the ones having their way with Horace. She'd given up on the microphone and was now using her youth-soccer-coach voice to focus everyone on the task at hand.

Realizing she had seconds not minutes before things would wrap up on their own, Leslie launched into a speech about 'how important all of our pets are' as if the previous ten minutes hadn't happened.

She spoke calmly, too calmly as if there was going to be long-term damage and possibly therapy for the Take Your Dog to Work Day organizer of organizers.

Horace had been batted around and pulled apart, but he was still there, looking straight ahead.

Chip picked him up when it was safe to do so, looked into his unblinking eyes, and thought, *this little guy is a survivor.*

Chapter 15

Collective Wisdom

It was early March and high time Chip paid a visit to his brother, Rick, who lived an hour south of him.

Chip's brother, Rick, was an army veteran who served two tours in Iraq and came home with minor PTSD. He wasn't about to go postal, but his anger simmered just below the surface, and most of the time Rick needed an outlet to get through life.

Online gaming was Rick's pressure-relief valve.

His connections with the online gaming community gave him access to the typical shoot 'em up team events. In these venues, too much thinking could get you off-ramped to a lower skill-level team.

In his virtual world, Rick tolerated just enough connection with others to feel part of something that would feed his appetite.

When the dreams came and the burn would start, he could go to his man cave, crank up his metal music, put on his virtual reality or VR headset, and enter a world he understood only too well.

Everyone had an itch to scratch and fighting the undead alongside fellow gamers was his itch. And that itch got scratched every day, sometimes twice, and never in the same place.

When Chip knocked on Rick's door, he made sure he called beforehand and then, at his house, gave the code in a foreign accent.

Rick felt an affinity for Guatemalans, so the accent had to be legit. The practice time getting the accent right was not bad because you spoke to Rich in short sentences and fewer syllables.

Rick was a conspiracy theorist which meant he believed someone or something was watching his movements every day and on weekends. You just couldn't be sure if someone was real or American, according to the world of Rick.

There was always that one person in the crowd – at the grocery store, in the mall, at the beach, in the library – who didn't look quite right, not quite there. Although Chip was Rick's brother, they always went through this elaborate authentication process before being allowed in. This time, he passed.

Rick was a source of strength for Chip. Rick had seen things and done things he didn't like to talk about, but Chip tried to pry anyway.

War stories were Chip's way to connect with his brother, a man of few words and even fewer possessions. From what could be gleaned, Rick was in special ops and had gone 'off the grid' a few too many times while 'in-country,' whatever and wherever that country was.

Once in a while, while sleeping over, Chip heard Rick talk in his sleep, an Arabic dialect that kept Chip up all night and wondering how much he really knew about his brother's military service.

Rick was in a relationship, albeit a long-distance one. There was a question whether his past relationship with an Iraqi girl had been sanctioned by the local cleric in eastern Baghdad, but the details were fuzzy. This haunted Chip.

He thought he would like to meet this mysterious woman who might help unlock some secrets about Rick. Maybe he would learn a little more about his brother, a little more about his past that was sealed shut and silent.

Rick's house was a minimalist's dream – the bare essentials. Rick was a man of simple tastes – a couch in the living room, a huge screen television mounted on the wall, and a gaming station and VR headset near a mini-fridge. When Chip said mini fridge, in this context, what he really meant was a small cooler.

The other rooms were equally sparsely decorated.

Rick didn't want unnecessary fluff and distractions in his life. Only one room, the living room, was carpeted. That room had special powers, according to Rick, and was his last resort when things got out of hand in other rooms. If he had a lifeline, it was only a Wi-Fi connection away.

Chip wanted to get advice on how he was supposed to get through cancer. Rick tackled life's challenges head-on and Chip admired him for that.

Rick had returned from Iraq with some aggression, especially when he drove. He had a short fuse and would drive against traffic just to change things up a bit. It was like Russian roulette on tarmac, but they always moved out of the way.

Rick entered the virtual world as a way to connect with others who walked a similar path and understood his fears. Rick knew what it meant to go in and out of the valley of death. So many close calls. Chip thought if anyone could help him tackle a breast-cancer diagnosis, it would be him.

Chip sought advice from Rick in the past but with varying degrees of success.

When Chip asked Rick for advice on how to better interact with females, Rick hadn't been gentle.

When Chip asked Rick for advice on where he should apply for college, Rick openly questioned higher education and then Chip.

One could feel Rick's concern and love but at the same time wonder if Rick was bored with the question and simply dispensed advice by reading verbatim from any one of the many unwrapped fortune cookies around the house. Rick loved Chinese food. B-grade, Chinese food reminded Rick of Bangkok in the '90s.

"Hi, Rick, how's your week been?" Chip asked. An innocent question, but Chip could never tell how it would go. Rick didn't do innocent.

"Okay, I guess." There was a brief pause.

"So, you have cancer! How bad?" Then, a longer pause while Chip was thinking about how to answer Rick's question.

"Lung or brain? It's usually the brain," Rick opined.

"Well, it's really kind of a mild cancer. Actually, I have breast cancer." Chip knew that was a curveball. He held his breath. He never knew how Rick would respond to things like men having breast cancer.

There was a flicker in Rick's eyes.

"Breast cancer?" Rick looked up from his comic book. *Chip looked on the weak side*, Rick thought. Rick was 42 years old, a comic-book aficionado, a chronic gamer, and a man trying to be in the present. Two out of three wasn't bad.

"Yes," said Chip.

"Men don't get breast cancer?" said Rick. It was a statement and a question.

"Uh, I do," said Chip. Chip wondered if he'd picked the right day to have this conversation. Tuesdays were usually better for Rick.

"You do?" Rick was puzzled. This was one of those moments when Rick knew he had to say something that only a big brother would say to a younger brother.

"Yes," said Chip. Chip wondered if he was beginning or ending a conversation with his aloof, distant, and damaged brother.

"Never heard of any man getting breast cancer. Didn't know that was a thing." Rick's time was equally divided between the floor, his comic book, and Chip's chest area.

It was likely the most eye contact Chip was going to get from Rick today.

"I need some advice. I know it's probably nothing. I mean I have to go through chemo and stuff. I know it will be tough. You know what tough is. Any advice?" "Chemo! Does Mom know?" said Rick, alarmed, ignoring Chip's request.

"It's just routine," Chip said, trying to be calm.

Better to be safe than sorry, Doctor Raj had told Chip that, but now he was beginning to wonder. *Maybe he'd rather be sorry*, Chip thought. Is that what a doctor says to all the men with breast cancer under their right nipple?

"Chemo on your breast? Which one?" asked Rick.

"The right one, right below the nipple," Chip explained. Then Chip spoke slowly, trying to mask his frustration, "I guess what I'm trying to say is do you have any ideas on how—"

Rick interrupted. "Take it one a day at a time. Live in the present. And consider avocados," Rick sounded strong, coherent, authoritative.

"Avocados?" *Was it really that simple?* Chip thought. "Nature's cure for all things evil. Listen, Bro. When I was over there (he meant Iraq) on my second tour, everyone, I mean everyone, forgot about us, and we had to assimilate, we had to mesh with the locals." Rick was on a roll.

"We were cut off for weeks. Nobody was coming in or out. Things started to slide, and I started to forget why I was there, why I wore the uniform.

"In one of my darkest moments, one of the street kids came up to me by our observation post and offered me an avocado." Rick leaned back.

It was Chip's turn to process and validate.

"Was it really an avocado? Or is the avocado a metaphor?" Chip asked.

"No, it was really an avocado, man. It was green, rippled, and..." Rick's speech was trailing like his attention span.

161

"Rick, you there?" Chip was getting worried again."Yeah, I'm fine. Yeah, that avocado did it for me. Snapped me back – got me refocused – gave me strength."

Rick wondered the last time he had grocery shopped for real fruits and vegetables. Typically, he would make a dash for the frozen food section, grab anything colored red or blue, and hurry back to his place before the next game started online.

"Okay, avocados it is. Anything else?" Chip would give it a try; why not?

"Life is an avocado, Bro!" Rick said, emphasizing the word avocado and downplaying 'bro' which hurt Chip a little.

Rick's slight smile quickly vanished. His gamer buddies would be waiting for him – they needed a fighting cleric with a gazillion life points to spare in an upcoming clash with the warlocks.

Rick hoped Chip would leave soon. His friends were pinging him and the game was starting with or without him in three minutes. The countdown was onscreen.

Chip got the hint and left. He thought he had what he needed from Rick to at least get through chemo in the right frame of mind.

He had a couple of avocados in his fridge, but he had bought them for Horace, his one and only pet tortoise. Sorry, Horace.

On his drive home, Chip thought about taking the next step into the great unknown with his cancer and giving therapy a go, group therapy.

He had been delaying going to one of those breast-cancer-support group meetings for a few good reasons and one terrible one.

Cancer was with him every day, always on his mind no matter how positive he tried to be or how much energy he tried to manufacture up to get him up and out.

Most days, if he were being honest, his cancer got the better of him, coaxing him to stay down and to stay away from people and things that would feel more connection and more support in this fight he was in.

Yes, if Chip was finally looking at himself in the mirror with the veneer, he could now say he was ready to open up and to share and to maybe help someone else feeling as low as he could get sometimes.

Part 4
The Best in Others

Chapter 16
All Things Pink

If there was one friend who was a flag-waving advocate of 'name your cause,' Janice was it. Her badges, trinkets, stickers, and mementos said everything you needed to know about this extreme extrovert who bounced from one cubicle to the next.

Always bubbly and out of breath, she promoted her *cause du jour* like there were three minutes left on the planet to tell you the most important thing you needed to hear before she spontaneously exploded.

Janice was the second woman in his life to suggest he join a breast-cancer-therapy group. Jillian in the MRI room had been the first and the suggestion had never left him.

Janice's insistence was overbearing, but he was used to it. As long as she didn't get inside his personal space, he could listen without getting fidgety.

When Janice heard about Chip's diagnosis, she became possessed, convinced that Chip should attend the support-group meetings and delve into the world of pink.

Janice was over by his cubicle, trying to convince him to give the group a try. She was half-smiling, half-selling.

"But I'm a guy, Janice; guys don't do breast-cancer-support groups!" Chip said. Janice was unmoved.

In reality, Chip had tried organized groups before, especially ones requiring vetting, but this breast-cancer group seemed an unlikely fit for Chip. On rare occasions (as in once a decade), he considered himself a rebel, up for something ground-breaking, even dangerous. Doing something like this would fall into that category of ventures.

Joining an all-women's therapy group, having to share feelings with others, now that was something truly upending for Chip. Didn't he need to be endorsed or something? Was his name 'put forward' by someone inside? He thought Janice may be the 'in.' She certainly had the *wasta* around the office.

"I've spoken to Claire," Janice reassured him. Chip thought the name Claire sounded safe, welcoming, whoever Claire was. "They meet tonight, in the cafeteria. Here's your shirt. Put it on, see how it fits."

She didn't leave. She waited for him to try it on.

Janice didn't have an inside voice; she had one volume and it was loud as if she had missed social cues from an early age. Chip's colleagues were listening. They imagined Chip in pink. They couldn't see it.

Janice was insistent. Gone was the bubbly, flighty Janice and, instead, with the pink shirt in hand, she could have been an army sergeant, ordering her recruits not to question but to follow obediently.

Chip knew that this was the first step in joining group therapy but putting on a pink shirt while others watched was pushing him into a corner.

As he put on the shirt, the small crowd of onlookers cheered the way a small group of accountants would cheer – a muted, desperate sound. Thankfully, the cheer was short-lived and Chip was left to wonder if pink was the new black and if Janice had a larger size.

He certainly looked different in pink. It wasn't a political statement; he just was just into bland colors. Still, in pink, he felt a kinship with others who wore pink, as if he was traveling on a path with other cancer-fighting crusaders.

He hadn't met anyone yet from the group but believed he had passed his first test. Janice looked on approvingly.

"The meeting is tonight at 7 p.m.," said Janice. "You're on your own, Chip. I'm not allowed in the group, only allowed to recruit. Let me know how it goes. Live long and prosper." She looked around to make sure no one was watching and then did the Vulcan sign that only Trekkies understood.

I knew it, Chip thought, *another closet Trekkie. They come in all shapes and sizes!* And then, she was gone, the sound of her trinkets trailing in the background as she bounced to another group of cubicles.

***

It was after hours in the building. The sun was setting and its final rays of light streamed through the cafeteria on the first floor.

The cafeteria was open for breakfast and lunch but not for dinner. Corporate chose not to offer three meals a day. They thought that sort of extravagance was encouraging the wrong behaviors. Now it was time for the cafeteria to serve a different purpose.

As they arrived and congregated around the snack tables, Chip noticed how self-assured they acted, so positive, friendly.

Everybody wore pink in some form of other, mostly with their pink shirts. Chip stayed back in the shadows while they all assembled in the cafeteria around a large circle of chairs. They were here for each other. That much he could discern.

There were plenty of hugs and there was plenty of pink. Everyone was female. Not a man in sight, except for Chip, off to the side, waiting for the right moment to introduce.

"Who are you?" the voice was edgy but gave an opening for leeway if a correct password was given.

"Hi. Janice said I could come. I'm Chip Clementine. Are you Claire? Janice said Claire said it would be okay if I came."

He felt like his whole life lay in balance over whether this woman knew Claire. *Why am I so quick to name-drop in unfamiliar settings?* Chip wondered.

"Oh, yeah. So, you're the one. Yes, I'm Claire. Well, I'm glad you made it, but there are some others who got wind of this and…" her voice trailed off as did her attention.

Someone had brought their famous spinach dip and announced it to the reception of whoops and hollers.

Claire grabbed Chip's arm and brought him out of the shadows and anonymity and toward the sea of pink. He didn't resist. He was pulled in.

He was warmly greeted by the people closest to him. There were stares, but, generally, he felt he was welcomed, though it did cross his mind that they may have him confused as a guest speaker rather than an initiate. He was shown to a seat.

There were two women, larger than most, who were fixated on him, eating their spinach dip and chips without breaking eye contact. There was no warmth in their eyes.

Chip wore his pink shirt with pride and silently declared that the spinach dip was superior to other spinach dips that he had sampled at work. What was the secret ingredient? he wondered.

Claire stood up and cleared her throat loudly.

"Everyone, attention please," Claire said loudly. "This is Chip. He's one of us. Let's bring it in and start this meeting off with a big group hug."

Claire was the clear leader of the group. Erect carriage, nametag written legibly, piercing but warm eyes. But Claire mentioned something about a hug and that sent shockwaves through Chip's frame.

Chip wasn't a fan of physical contact. When he was pulled into the group, he was smothered in a sea of pink and hair.

He'd never been comfortable touching other people. It wasn't them; it was him. He knew it. It was a thing for him.

As twenty or so women hugged him, he imagined each person had a communicable disease. He knew his asthma inhaler was close by, but he couldn't have gotten to if he tried.

As a young boy, he could tell what people had eaten by smelling their breath even though they were yards away. He wasn't proud of this, but it had come in handy during family get-togethers when someone had to break the ice and get people laughing.

A couple of them took the bait of the spinach dip; that was easy. He could tell that others were juicers/smoothers – dedicating their lunch meal to anything liquefied down to the bare essentials.

He was sure some calorie counted but most cheated, evidenced by a few with hints of a chocolaty peanut-butter bar on their breath.

He couldn't be sure, but he also thought there were some on the periphery who had just downed some peppermint candies like the world was ending and that was all there was to eat. Chip had some unique skills and talents that he kept mostly to himself.

He kept his eyes closed as everyone kept closed in around him. Chip went to his safe place which was thinking about glamping in a national park out west. And then it was over. He felt the release.

He was helped back to his seat by Claire. She then took a breath and looked around the room with a smile that said 'settle down, ladies' and looked at Chip, the only man in pink, clearly flushed. Claire continued with the introduction/indoctrination of Chip, "Chip, why don't you tell us where you're at in your journey? Take your time. Everyone is on their own journey. We're here to support each other. And we think it's wonderful that we have our first man in our group, don't we, ladies?"

Muted applause.

Chip wasn't sure if the applause was more about deference and respect for Claire or a genuine welcome to a new member. Still, the vibe was good enough for him to open up.

Just when Chip was about to speak up, a voice from the outer ring of this trust circle beat him to it. Her name was Alexis, and she had an ax to grind on Chip.

"I don't see why 'he' has to be here. This is about women, not men. This is about breast cancer," her voice had an edge.

"We don't get to have much of our own things anymore, and this group is about the only one left. I mean, they are everywhere."

Despite the bite in her voice, Chip appreciated the clarity of thought and the honesty but not the way she hissed out her words. Fortunately, Chip had an ally in the room, and that ally's name started with 'C' and ended with 'laire.'

"Now, Alexis, calm down," Claire acted like she said this to Alexis all the time.

"Chip is suffering just like all of us. Breast cancer isn't just for women; men have it too. Chip is the first man I know with it, but he has every right to be part of our group." Others in the room listened intently.

"Now, unless you wish to invoke the challenge, then I suggest you come over here and give Chip a big hug and ask him to tell us his story."

Alexis didn't move at first, but when she did, she moved quickly across the room and toward Chip, again the fixed stare. She never blinked!

In three bounding steps, she was staring down at him, not more than six inches from his face. Her breath was one-hundred percent spinach dip – breakfast, lunch, and dinner.

"I invoke the challenge, Claire. Right here, right now."

There were immediate protests from the others as if this was totally uncalled for, inappropriate even. But someone did whoop.

Claire had to respect the ground rules even if she didn't embrace all of them. Clearly surprised that Alexis hadn't backed down, Claire scanned the room and then looked at Chip.

"Chip, you have your rights, and we do respect the challenge."

Claire had reluctantly become an umpire of sorts. What the heck is 'the challenge?' Chip was so confused but cognizant that no one had offered him food yet.

Claire continued, "Chip, we have some strange rules in our group, but they're approved and seconded as part of our charter.

"The challenge has been issued by Alexis. It looks like you'll arm wrestle Alexis for the right to enter the group. I was hoping it would not come to this, but, well, here we go."

Claire shrugged her shoulders like this had happened before and that once in a while, membership was decided by physical force.

And just like that, Claire was pushed aside by associates of Alexis, three equally large women who were there to perform crowd-control duties. The rest of the group formed around the small table hastily pushed to the middle of the room.

Chip was still taking this in. An arm wrestle? Are they serious? Claire had a resigned look on her face as if she didn't approve but couldn't go against the rules. She was bound by tradition and perhaps precedent to not interfere.

Chip had never arm-wrestled in his life mostly because it likely involved sweating. Chip didn't like to sweat.

He could tell you what it was. He thought it was a sport in the last century or two but not in the modern era. And certainly didn't think arm-wrestling happened in therapy groups. Who made that one up?

Two camps quickly formed – the pro-Alexis crowd and everybody else. Chip thought he heard someone's iPhone playing provocative music like it was egging Alexis on. No need for music, Alexis was already egged on.

The betting started immediately. It was clear that Chip was not the favorite. He saw dollar bills thrown around like candy. Still, when the bell rang from another's iPhone, it was over before it began.

Alexis was all talk and no muscle. They locked hands in identical grips, although she had nails, long ones. When the bell went off, Alexis drove Chip's hand down toward her, pulling him in.

Chip felt a rush, a source of strength that came from a place he hadn't felt since eighth grade when ninth-grader and school bully, Austin Boland, decided that his own lunch was not filling enough and maybe someone else's, like Chip's, would fill him up.

It was in that small cafeteria that Chip found that a few choice words coupled with a physical gesture or two could stand down the bulliest of bullies.

Austin didn't get Chip's lunch that day, but he did get a new measure of respect for someone he had marked as easy prey.

In the desperate seconds of the arm wrestle, Chip summoned that same strength and adrenalin from all those years ago, and he slowly pulled his hand back toward him, looking at Alexis as her confidence faded and imminent defeat loomed large.

Chip drove her hand down and the cries from the crowd reached a deafening crescendo. Alexis, surprisingly, took it well – too well.

She looked up at Chip from the floor in humiliation and blinked. "You're one of us now, Chip."

There was another group hug and, this time, all Chip could smell was three equal parts of acceptance, inclusion, and spinach dip.

Chapter 17

The Dead of Winter

It was late March and the cold slowed everything down. Each had their own way of coping. Chip was no different.

January and February were the months when he would hibernate, insulate himself from others as if he were saving his energy, his soul for better use in the months to come. But his factory-default settings for those winter months could not have come at a worse time.

He delayed the start of his chemotherapy until after Christmas and had pushed it off even further until February. Here he was, desperate for the month to be over. It had been hard.

Finishing up his first round of chemotherapy, which consisted of no less than eight sessions, he was ten pounds heavier, had lost his appetite for savory snacks, and felt the effects of gravity more acutely than ever before.

The weight gain was expected – the lapses into sheer terror and hopelessness were not. His company gave him liberal sick leave to receive his treatment.

Chemotherapy in layman's terms was when drugs entered the body to kill cells without discrimination to shrink, slow, and stop any cancer cells. Of course, normal cells were also fair game.

Invasive drugs going into his body terrified him. And, now, after two rounds of chemo, he still hadn't accepted that these drugs were his friends.

There were some nights when he would wake up fully aware he was a cancer patient and nothing else. In the stillness of the night, he would slowly get out of bed, careful not to wake Mrs. Clementine, and walk down the creaky stairs to his study where he contemplated his life in an attempt to extract meaning from it.

Not surprisingly, he would recount some of the bigger mistakes in his life which only amplified his feelings of regret and remorse.

He knew this was a downward spiral and would spend many hours in that room reliving moments when he could have built stronger ties with those he cared about.

In this melancholic state, his worst regrets were those where he had, through his actions, distanced himself from some family members. He would think a lot about his sister, Janice, but not for too long. It was too painful.

It usually took three days after the clinic visit before the drugs' effects would arrive violently and abruptly on Chip's biological doorstep. Thinking about their imminent arrival drove up his anxiety.

The first round of chemo when the drugs hit his system the first time was the worst because he didn't know what to expect, despite what others had told him.

After the first chemo session, he knew what to expect. The weight gain was gradual and steady – no surprise there.

The hair coming out was anti-climactic; he already had a thinning hairline and preemptively shaved his head without fuss or fanfare. Secretly, he'd always wanted to give it a go and wondered why he hadn't done it years ago.

He looked good bald, so he thought. But the big surprise was the fatigue. He would get so tired that he would have trouble speaking as if mouthing the words required energy that he just didn't have.

He slept a lot, maybe too much. At least when he slept, he didn't have to think about his mortality. Some days were a blur, but others would be punctuation marks in seismic, life-changing ways, usually when people visited him.

A week after his first round, new friends from the cancer-support group visited him.

There was Claire, of course, her nameless deputy (didn't know cancer-support-group leaders had deputies), and Alexis who had challenged him to a ritualistic contest during his first group meeting. They showed with pink shirts and smiles to spare.

They came into his bedroom, grabbed chairs, and spent an hour or so talking about positive things, things that made him laugh and forget he was in bed, immobile and dependent on others.

They talked about their treatment and their symptoms. On the face of it, one would think such talk would push Chip further along the train tracks of human despair. But hearing his friends talk about their own treatments and found ways to cope gave him the lift he needed for the day.

The talking was nice and should have been enough, but it wasn't for them. They insisted on watching any cry-worthy movies on the Hallmark Movie Channel that had a predictable and happy ending. Others visited him during this colder, darker January – each for their own reasons and with their own ways of loving and supporting Chip.

His brother, Rick, stopped by a few times – every Thursday since Thursdays were his designated break days from gaming with his online friends. If he and his buddies were to stay mentally fit, they knew they should engage with the live world at least one day a week to avoid assuming their avatar characters.

Rick wasn't much of a talker; two tours in Iraq turned him more inward than outward. But Rick knew how to play the guitar and he didn't ask for permission to play. He just started playing mid-conversation.

Rick strummed and sang a rock ballad that made Chip wonder if music therapy was covered by insurance. Chip never stopped admiring Rick's patience though. In between vomiting spells, Rick would stop mid-chord, while Chip did his thing, only to pick up at the exact part in the ballad where he left off.

Chip was on the fence about the live music but felt loved and supported. And that was enough. Well, it had to be. Rick's ballad was two verses and that was it. He was out the door and onto his next gig or game.

The big surprise of the month had to be the unfortunate souls he had played pranks on with the nap pod-chair. They arrived with linked arms.

William, Ted, and LaTisha had been victims (strong word but accurate) of Chip's tampering with the pod chairs. Apparently, management found out about Chip's misadventures with the pod chairs and quietly approached each of them shortly thereafter. Chip was not contacted for unknown reasons.

All three were given certain inducements to keep quiet and only William had pushed back for more concessions. He had gotten all that was offered and then some.

All three had formed a loose friendship of sorts, the kind you can only have through a shared, traumatic experience. And now they were all crammed in Chip's bedroom, knees touching, and holding hands.

They were to the point. They'd written a poem together, a poem of healing and forgiveness.

LaTisha read the poem. It was only right that she should be the one to read it. In essence, the poem was more of a melodic chant followed by some clicks and heel tapping.

Words would not do justice to what they had been through, what they had overcome, so some light banging against Chip's bedpost was in order.

They knew what had happened and they forgave him. Chip was speechless and knew he had too many pillows propped up. He wanted to sink into those pillows the more they spoke.

LaTisha was especially moving as she had experienced the most physically jarring prank, being dropped out of the nap pod chair from a height of ten feet onto padded mats.

She told Chip that after a few therapy sessions, her therapist had helped her work through her feelings she felt after her 'drop.'

She came out of therapy grateful for the experience which had empowered her to accept randomness and unpredictability in life and enjoy the things that can be controlled.

After she learned Chip's role in her nap-pod nightmare, which wasn't until much later when she heard about Chip's cancer, she decided to visit him in his 'hour of need' and thank him.

All three, in their own way, thanked Chip, forgave Chip, and encouraged him to do likewise – let things go, Chip, things you cannot control. Focus on what you can do and you can do good for others.

It was a powerful message, and Chip wondered how much they needed to each to get to that point in their lives when they could let go of things when they could forgive others.

Management paid a visit, but it didn't feel like it was forced. Susan and Jeffrey came together – a united front. Jeffrey was clearly uncomfortable. He cracked his neck way too often.

He was Chip's first-line supervisor with the most knowledge of Chip's past indiscretions, misjudgments, and idiosyncrasies. But he was there, and Chip felt that Jeffrey wanted to be there, although he did trail Susan into the room and finished her sentences.

This was not Susan's first home visit to a sick employee. She did the talking.

They missed him. They missed his quirkiness, and they missed the effect he had on the other staff, especially during crunch times at the end of the month when reports were due. They were looking forward to Chip returning to the fourth-floor and planned to throw a big welcome back party/potluck for him.

Since the start of his sick leave three weeks ago, Susan assured him his cubicle had not been reassigned nor had his personal things been touched. Someone did turn off his computer monitor – energy conservation means cost savings – every little bit helps, they said. Chip couldn't argue with that. The logic worked.

Others visited. Some brought flowers because they didn't know what else to bring and felt stronger somehow walking into the home with a prop.

Chip's best friend, Jimbo, knew what to bring. He was nobody's fool and had convinced Jeffrey, both Chip's and Jimbo's manager, for him take the afternoon off to visit a co-worker – he left the best friend part off (thought it would distract Jeffrey).

Purely on humanitarian grounds, Jimbo picked up the most carb-loaded pizza he could imagine, which was no more than two toppings, and showed up on Chip's doorstep with sausage and pepperoni smells wafting out of the box and into the hallway.

Jimbo was easy company, mostly because it took a while for both to polish off the extra-large extravaganza of all-things meat, cheese, and tomato sauce.

There was nothing remotely close to thin-crust about Jimbo's lunch or Jimbo. Jimbo had no other friends, so having Chip out of commission for most of January was soul-crushing.

They relived their funnier moments together, played some backgammon, and strategized potential schemes to make things more interesting and less mundane on the fourth-floor when Chip returned.

Jimbo knew when he had overstayed his welcome – that was easy. When the last slice was gone and the two-liter soda drained empty, Jimbo knew they had spent quality time together.

Some of the younger crowd stopped by. Clarisse was a surprise. After the karaoke incident, he wasn't sure how to relate to someone who had questioned so harshly his singing talent.

Still, there she was, in his home, smiling and wishing him well. She seemed a little too much with her urging him to get better and return to the karaoke gigs. Maybe he would reserve the first song for her when he got back 'onstage,' she said.

Justin stopped by. His smile was infectious. Chip could tell the paper cuts from his neck had largely gone except for some of the bigger ones which looked like they were going to stay for a while.

Justin was an office celebrity because of his resilience in surviving repeated mini-avalanches of forgotten print jobs that crashed into his cubicle. He had the cuts, bruises, and scars to show his mettle, but he didn't brag and that is what made his stock soar. Such a bundle of positivity! Justin was good at small talk and Chip was fine with that.

Justin's latest project was building a retaining wall in his backyard and he spent more than a minute describing in detail each step of his winter project. Chip's first thought was that who organizes their projects by season?

Chip's next thought lasted a bit longer which was surprise at how a Zoomer worked outside, in the elements doing manual labor. Justin was shooting holes all day long in how Chip stereotyped this younger generation. Maybe he was wrong stereotyping the junior accountants?

Then there was John. Chip was surprised when he came to visit. John was married to Claire, the cancer-therapy-group leader. He had met him at a group meeting when everyone had brought in their spouse/ partner/significant other for a mini-social.

John was all the right adjectives – friendly, agreeable, positive, encouraging. He was so nice, he didn't seem real. He would listen intently, like he cared about what they had to say.

John was always smiling, even when no one was watching. During the mini-social (as opposed to a full-blown social), he smiled the whole time like smiling was his default expression.

The John smile was a smile that said here I am, there you are and that's okay with me! John didn't have much to say other than the smile which worked its magic. Chip felt happier around someone like John and a little more curious too. Chip wanted to ask him some questions.

John had come on his own to visit Chip. After more small talk, Chip saw an opening. "John, I wanted to ask you a weird question."

"Oh, go ahead." John was still smiling, but his manicured hands did loosen their grip on the chair.

"Why are you so happy all the time?" Chip asked. There was a pause. John held eye contact with Chip for longer than most would consider normal.

Chip was used to no-blink contests so could tolerate the elapsed stare time.

"Well, I guess I feel blessed, really blessed," John said.

"Yeah, but why do you feel blessed?"

"I feel blessed because God places me in situations all the time where I'm able do things for others, to give them a lift in some way, to help them feel loved."

These words, this language, was natural for John. He was a simple man with a simple message for anyone that would listen. Most did.

"Loved? So, you have a positive outlook on life because you help others feel more love in their life? Why do you do this?"

"Great question. I like living my life this way because I feel great inside when I am able to help others." There were other things that were said that morning, but that part of the conversation stuck with Chip. Blessed? God? Loved?

Chip knew he was getting what John was saying on a superficial level and that he would think more on their conversation later. But what he heard intrigued him.

John seemed a legitimately nice guy – someone who didn't seem to want personal gain at the expense of others. He was quite different from so many other people.

Later that evening in his bedroom, with both of his matching nightlights emitting their soft glows on either side of his bathroom door, Chip's mind began to wander.

It'd been so long since he had done something completely selfless in his life, done something for someone else without any expectation of reward, payback, recompense.

He knew something had happened to him when he was a kid, but it had been so long ago. When was it? Where was it? Something to do with a candy store.

And then the memory came flooding back. He was five years old and he had some loose change in his pocket.

It wasn't very often others gave him money to buy candy, but when it happened, it was a chance to buy happiness from his local general store.

As a five-year-old, Chip's life boiled down to the essentials, playing pick-up games in the neighborhood with assorted street urchins, like himself, being fed at scheduled times of the day and occasionally being given license to go to the neighborhood store and buy sweets.

The store sold many things which surprised Chip because the entire floor dimensions of the store were approximate to a small living room in someone's house, but without a sofa.

An elderly gentleman was the owner and would barely register Chip and the other boys as they entered his establishment, intent on sizing up their buying options with the loose change someone had given them as well.

What was clear was that the store stacked one type of merchandise over all others – candy. Not just chocolate, and not just wrapped confectionary, but even the hard, sweet, and savory candy that took an hour to be sucked down to a manageable level before being digested.

Chip and the other kids figured out quickly that sugar highs lasted longer with hard candy and every bit of loose change would be spent on it.

Some of his friends had a different strategy, falling for the allure of all things chocolate, but they were the first to whine and beg for one of Chip's gobstoppers when they burned through their own stash.

The five-minute walk to the store was plenty of time for Chip to burn mental cycles, calculating and recalculating.

These were precious moments for him as he went through the what-ifs, the contingencies in case his first choice selections were not available for purchase.

There was a time, Chip recalled looking back all those years later, when he showed up to the store only to find that none of his go-to selections were in stock and watched helplessly as friends scooped up other candy options while Chip felt like he was in quicksand, helpless and unable to move.

That was the time he committed to never engage in any enterprise without a viable Plan B.

There were no guarantees when it came to how much loose change might be handed to him by a close family member. It was a real coin toss (pun intended) if you were given enough money to buy the right kind of hard candy that would last the afternoon and into the evening.

Chip's memory focused on one of those summer afternoons when his granddad, feeling especially generous, unloaded both his pockets of change into Chip's grateful hands.

His sister, Jen, was nearby and saw everything. This wasn't the first time he would need to fend off her attempts to crash an imminent candy-buying party, so he was quick and to the point. Chip would do her chores for a week and no more.

Chip's walk to this store was less a purposeful stroll and more a spiritual pilgrimage. He was never so loaded down with money, mostly pennies and a smattering of dimes.

He knew there were quarters in there somewhere but wanted them to show up when the old guy at the store would ask for payment and he could dump it all out on the counter and would see the old man's surprise.

The possibilities were endless with the amount he likely had in his pockets.

He arrived at the store in a dream state, like he could see himself entering his favorite place and heading straight to the rows and rows of hard candies piled several feet high in clear, plastic jars so high that only adults could reach.

Inside the store, looking up and down and through these jars, Chip estimated the combinations, types, and weights he would buy. Nothing was more important to his five-year-old mind than getting this right. And then he saw them, out of the corner of his eye.

Two elderly, frail-looking ladies weighed down with groceries walked slowly toward the store, his store.

As they waddled, struggled their way toward the door, Chip experienced his first moral quandary, his first set of conflicting thoughts as he rounded out his five years on earth and stared down first grade that fall.

As they approached, Chip felt something. It was hard to explain, but he knew the right thing to do was to open the door for those old ladies.

No one was telling him he had to do it. He had clarity of thought at that moment, a moment that was coming back to Chip all those years later.

No one was telling him he had to open that door. There were no competing voices in his head. There were no angles to work or deals to be struck. There was no advantage to be gained at another's expense.

He would open the door just because it was the right thing to do and he wouldn't worry or concern himself with what would happen next.

In one bound, he was at the door. He opened it wide just as the two old ladies came up to the front of the store. They were surprised, but their surprised looks turned to warm smiles as they looked at Chip. They thought they had seen him before. Probably had.

He was always in a crowd, but today he was no longer part of a crowd to them. He was quite remarkable.

"Thank you, Sonny," they both said in unison and slowly walked through the doorstep into Chip's store.

The shop owner greeted two of his favorite patrons and hadn't noticed a young boy doing something remarkable for someone else, an act of kindness that would stay buried in Chip's memory only to resurface much later because others chose to do something for him he could not do for himself.

Chip remembered more about that time. He remembered how he felt when those ladies, weighed down with their own concerns that hot, summer day, were helped by someone they didn't expect to help them. Chip was given a gift that day.

The gift of kindness he experienced was that he had put something or someone above his own interests, cares, and concerns.

He'd opened a door into a bigger, better Chip.

It wasn't too late for him to open more doors for others, he thought, even as he suffered through chemo sessions and wondered if there was more he could offer to others.

Chapter 18

Blueberries over Waffles

Chip didn't believe in coincidences, fate, or serendipity, especially serendipity.

Last year, Mrs. Clementine convinced him to watch the movie of the same name, more on a dare, and it hadn't worked out well. Chip didn't like the acting, the mispronunciations, and canned dialogue.

The movie failed his logic tests for movies on so many levels. His wife's attempts to salvage the movie night with popcorn that was nuked a little too long was an epic fail and only cemented his anti-serendipitousness. If he wasn't then, he certainly was, now, a flag-waving, radical believer in chance and random encounters.

And then John came into his life. There was no way that was chance.

When John stopped by Chip's house that pivotal week in March during his recuperation, John said things that had evoked strong memories of an earlier time in Chip's life when he experienced a truly unique event – Chip performing a singular act of kindness without any thought of reward.

He remembered what he felt, how he felt, and wanted to feel more of whatever that was in his life, especially now.

Three days later, Chip and John sat across from each other in a small, cozy diner. Each looked at their plastic breakfast menus but were both thinking of other things besides breakfast.

Chip knew he was going to order the waffles and was thinking about how this was going to go down. Chip had asked for the meeting and John guessed at the reasons why. Chip spoke first, and when he did, it was fast, really fast.

"The waffles are amazing. You should try them. They come with blueberries, but they're always mushy. I just tell them 'no fruit' in case someone in the back gets offended that I singled out blueberries. It's easier to swallow, if you're the blueberry guy, when someone says they don't want fruit, right?"

Chip was nervous, and when he was nervous, he talked fast.

Chip struggled with small talk. He wasn't a small talker, wasn't a big talker. Any kind of talking beyond a certain point took too much effort and he knew it.

He preferred to save his strength until a small or big talker gave him an opening, usually an intake of breath. Without those openings, Chip would bide his time and try more creative ways to get things back on track, his track.

Creative was hard, and exhausting. So, Chip went down the creative path with blueberries and waffles.

Chip assumed John was a waffles fan – fruit or no fruit. John wasn't but went with it because that's how John was around others – the consummate accommodator, the pleaser's pleaser. Waffles would suit him just fine, John thought to himself. And, sure, why not blueberries since we're here and Chip is probably paying since he called the meeting.

John looked forward to being with Chip, just like he looked forward to, pretty much, being with anyone. John found every single human being on the planet incredibly interesting.

So, there they were. Chip and John across from each other, having just ordered waffles with no fruit.

Chip spoke first, "Thanks for meeting me here. I come here a lot. Some people do their best thinking walking in a park, sitting in a library, showering. I can think through things better here than anywhere else for some strange reason."

Chip smiled inside. This was really some pretty good small talk. He kept going. John was listening, not distracted and focused his deep blue eyes on Chip without judgment.

"After we spoke the other day, I remembered something that happened to me as a kid. I helped someone, actually two old ladies. I remembered how I felt when I helped them. It's been a while since I felt like that. I think I need more of that in my life now, especially lately with what I have been dealing with."

"It feels great to do something nice for someone, right?" John figured they would be talking about something like this.

"It does, but it seems like all my life I've been connecting what I do to a reward, something that helps me get something or somewhere. It's always seemed…conditional. It's embarrassing to talk about, but I've always expected something back," said Chip.

"I know what you mean. I used to be like that when I was younger. Everything was give and take, this for that," John replied.

John knew exactly when his 'younger' happened and also when it stopped happening. His dad, a career police officer in a town like this one, died suddenly of a heart attack when he was in high school, leaving behind a devastated wife and seven children. John was the oldest of the seven. After that day, he needed to worry about more important things than himself.

The waffles arrived…with blueberries dropped on the waffles with a vengeance, like the guy in the back had overhead them and decided on double the portion of blueberries for the two guys speaking ill of blueberries.

The blueberries guy, knowing at least one of the group was a regular, would dare Chip into eating his blueberries and not causing affront to the staff who had served him all these years in good faith.

Thankfully, the blueberries guy was not another type of guy, like a breadfruit guy where only a certain palate could stomach that type of fruit on anything, especially waffles.

Blueberries would work, they would have to for today. No, Chip imagining what the blueberries guy was thinking that morning, they (Chip and John) would grow to love blueberries and the diner is where it would happen.

The blueberries guy was looking at them from his back work-area. Johnny, the short order cook, stopped the bacon fry just to see Chip's reaction.

Alice, the waitress, looked over at their table mid-stream of taking an order from some other regulars. Chip knew what was happening.

They looked at each other, shrugged their shoulders, and both took a bit from their plates. Good conversation would have to help them navigate through mushy blueberries on waffles for now – it was that or choose another diner. They kept talking.

They were here for the waffles; everything was okay. They were in a safe space.

This diner was about as safe a place as Chip could want for progressing awkward conversations with someone like John. Chip had been coming here for years and loved everything about it, except the sticky seats.

Time had stopped by in the early '80s and never left. The diner served breakfast, lunch, and dinner seven days a week without fail.

It was the only local hangout in this part of town and served up the usual stereotypes and clichés. Alice, the only waitress there in the postage-stamp-sized diner, was in her mid-60s and it showed. She started there out of high school and never looked back.

Alice was a local girl and couldn't imagine living anywhere else, anywhere away from friends she had grown up with and a tight-knit family that had been part of this blue-collar town for generations.

Working at the diner had ticked many of Alice's boxes over the years – the place where she met her ex-husband, fell in and out of love, raised two kids as a single mom, and scraped up enough tip money to buy a small place of her own.

After the divorce, it was enough for Alice to come home to her apartment, happily single, to her three cats who she adored so much and whose names and faces were prominently tattooed on the back of her calves – two on one and one on the other. The other was her favorite, but she didn't tell the other two.

The diner was an extension of Alice, or was it the other way round? The diner had its own identity – stale advertisements posted on the walls, black-and-white chequered linoleum and long-since retired and commercially unavailable for purchase.

There was the smell of bacon everywhere, coffee-stained, local newspapers tossed around several tables, cracked, red leather barstools with no backs, and, of course, the jukebox that only took quarters and only played what your parents liked or maybe your grandparents liked.

The owners framed their first dollar bill a customer had given them when they opened the diner right about the time Alice graduated high school and was looking for work. The frame was next to larger one of Alice with the owners celebrating their first year in business.

People felt comfortable in the diner because Alice always remembered their names and made them feel like they were in her home. They felt safe. And when people felt safe, they tipped.

Alice had a good heart, but she never forgot what she did for others and how there was a big difference between tipping amounts and what made the difference between the two.

She did what she could to make her customers feel safe, connected, and whatever else they felt they needed to get the extra income she needed.

Tips were not appreciated in this diner, they were expected. Her cats were part of her family, and cat food was expensive.

"How's it going, Chip? You liking those blueberry waffles?" said Alice. There she was, energized. She was only into the first two hours of her shift and already pocketed twenty dollars in tips. Chip would, no doubt, add to her good fortune this morning. He could always be counted on for a decent tip.

She was perky, but it was an act and she fooled everyone, even Chip. She was not a morning person, so the smile evaporated when no one was watching, usually when she returned to the bar area and restocked plastic straws or pretended to read the newspaper.

The paper was a smart move since no one smiled reading this town's paper, especially the obituaries which she read like she couldn't get enough of them.

The newspaper was almost entirely funded by paid obituaries. There were more people dying than living apparently.

If people didn't die, and obituaries weren't written, the breakfast regulars would have nothing to talk about, except which one of them might be next, Chip thought.

Maybe that is what the 'gang of five' did every morning instead of reading the newspaper obituaries – just sit around and critique their own and their buddies' obituaries, as if they could change their past.

Chip snapped back to his table and Alice leaning over him with that smile again. "Absolutely delicious! Was this Johnny's idea?" Johnny had been around as long as Alice.

Chip was convinced they were both in on any number of schemes, blueberries on waffles being the latest, to get as much extra tips out of customers as possible without them noticing or being duped.

"How'd you guess? Glad you like 'em," Alice said. "He wanted to do a something different with the blueberries. Can you taste the cinnamon?" There was that intense look again matched with a pursed smile.

Chip couldn't hesitate. She would see right through him. It hadn't happened yet, but there was always a first time. "Oh, yeah. Now I can. Where did he come up with that?" He had to look interested for everyone's sakes.

"Johnny's been reading up on stuff, recipes. If you like 'em, let me know. You know what I mean?" She looked at him intently, searching for any mental break. He gave her no such pleasure. He knew what she meant.

A good tip meant all was well between Chip, the diner, and Alice. He had always stayed in her good graces but knew that one faux-pas and it was a rapid descent from specially made blueberry waffles to scrambled eggs – no butter, salt, or pepper.

He would be shelling out a few more dollars in gratuities this morning.

He looked down at his barely eaten waffles and then up again. She was gone. How she had moved the 50 feet from their window table and onto the next customer at the other end of the diner, without him seeing her leave, was mystifying. And yet there she was, talking it up with another regular, angling for more cat-food money and maybe her next Caribbean cruise.

Chip turned back to John. Chip liked to watch people when they didn't notice. John was gazing out of the window in his own thoughts.

The blueberry waffles had been wolfed down and his glass was emptied. He was feeling the slight creases in the plastic menu that doubled as a placemat.

"Did you know this is my second round of chemo?" John asked like someone would ask if they had seen a mutual friend recently.

Chip had no idea. Claire told him about her husband's fight with lung cancer, but it was usually couched in a way that led Chip to believe John had beaten it and was now dutifully supporting his wife's passion for cancer-therapy groups since retiring from the town's police department.

Claire said John was medically retired but did not elaborate. Chip wanted Claire to elaborate. John was a walking mystery to be unpacked.

"No, I thought you had beaten it and were done?" said Chip with a suddenly dry mouth. Chip took a polite sip of orange juice.

"Well, my cancer seems to be sticking around, so the doctors recommended another round. Easy for them to say, right?" said John, looking down at his waffles.

It was a sarcastic comment about doctors who everyone thought never got cancer like the rest of us. But John's face didn't show sarcasm, just continual buoyancy, like he rode above what normal people's reactions would be to bad news.

Chip couldn't let it go. Was John permanently injured in the line of duty, fighting off street thugs in a back alley while the rest of us went about our lives, going to diners and ordering waffles, with or without blueberries?

Was John the hero Chip wished he could have been, even with the asthma condition?

"But you seem so positive all the time? How do you do it?" said Chip, perplexed.

"That's easy," John said. "My day is better when I think less about myself, my issues, my problems, and more about someone else. When I am less inward-focused and more outward-focused, I receive such a lift, Chip."

John spoke in such a confident manner, Chip noticed. *Where does he get it from? 'A lift?' That was an interesting way to put it*, Chip thought.

John continued, "Remember how you felt when you helped those two old ladies when you were younger? Well, you can feel that way every day; anyone can. Have you thought about that? I try to feel that way every day. I need that boost, that high to get me through the day, and some of my days would be pretty rough without love I feel from others."

This was deep, Chip thought.

They hardly knew each other, but Chip felt that John wasn't one for small talk either and just got straight to the point, like he didn't have much time left to spend with someone before needing to impart wisdom somewhere else.

Well, Chip thought, *here we are in my diner and I can see all the exits. Maybe there can be a little more sharing and a little less pretending.*

"How do you feel love from others?" Chip said.

There was no hesitation in the response. "I think it's really God's love for me that I feel. I'm not a churchy person, but I do believe in him, that he is real and that he knows who I am."

John drank some water, not because he had to but because he knew he had said a lot and wanted it to sink in.

"And because we all have a God, we all belong to the same human family; we are all connected somehow. I believe we are all connected as a human family, that we are all each other's brother or sister."

He paused, but only briefly.

"Everyone I meet is my brother and sister, so to speak, because we all have the same God who loves us. I feel his love in my life when I help my brothers and sisters. Does that make sense?"

John wanted Chip to understand what he was sharing. John was trying to say things, hard things, to a relative stranger. He had been in diners like this before with other Chips. He hoped Chip was getting it.

Chip was getting it…slowly. All Chip could think about was whether John had carefully developed this harmonious approach to life as a hard-nosed, street cop on the streets of his town or later in life as a retired man of leisure, albeit a cancer-stricken one.

"I've never really thought about other people like that before. If everyone around me is part of my extended family, I would certainly treat them differently, certainly better. So, when you help someone out, are kind to someone, how exactly do you feel?"

"I feel stronger, kinder, more powerful in a good way. I am more resilient, like I can handle what is thrown my way.

"I feel like I am force for good in this world and that it feels really good inside when I can help someone, especially when I can do something for someone else that they cannot otherwise do for themselves."

John spoke in soft tones, "I also feel loved, Chip. I feel that a lot of times I am put in a particular situation and given so many opportunities to be that person at the right place at the right time for someone else. I bet you felt like that when you were younger in that store, right?"

"I think a five-year-old doesn't think like that," said Chip dryly. "But I did feel better about myself. I remember that very clearly."

John went on, "Imagine if you could have those feelings every day in your life. I try to do something kind for someone else every day, not because I have selfish motives to feel better than someone else or anything like that.

"I do it because it is the right thing to do and because it feels so good to be able to give someone else a lift."

"I don't know if I can be like you," said Chip, somewhat dejectedly. The distance between them seemed vast.

"You don't have to be like me. Just be a better you," John said optimistically. Chip still wasn't convinced.

"Some people really bug me, John," said Chip. "How can you be nice to them?"

It was a valid question. "Some people are harder to love than others," John said with a smile. "Maybe they need your help more than the nicer ones?"

Alice seemed to sense when their conversation had reached a culminating point and slowly walked over with the bill and a couple of mints – her signature move.

John insisted on paying and Chip noticed that he left a twenty-dollar bill after he paid with his credit card.

"That was quite a tip. Alice will love you forever!" Chip said.

John was quick with the reply, "You never know what someone is going through. If I can make someone's day, give someone a lift, I will."

And, with that, they shook hands and promised to meet up again, maybe next month – same time same place but, hopefully, without the canned fruit. Those blueberries were mushy for no other reason than that.

John had made Alice's day with that tip. She could count on two hands and a couple of more fingers how many tips she had gotten over the years of that amount and more.

For the rest of the day, Alice found it a lot easier to smile, especially at the grumpy ones. Funnily enough, some of them smiled back…for the first time.

She would tell her cats all about the blue-eyed, tanned friend of Chip's later on tonight.

Chip turned a ten-minute drive home into a 30-minute drive home as he thought long and hard about what John said in the diner.

He liked what he heard. He knew John was deeply religious; Chip wasn't. He didn't know John was also in his second round of chemo but for an entirely different kind of cancer.

Chip's foray into chemotherapy had been rough, jolting, jarring. He didn't know how anyone could be so positive having to go through this again. But John said things that resonated with Chip.

Chip wasn't religious per se; he didn't go to church, say prayers, read the Bible, etc., but he did believe in God, that someone up there was bigger than all of him and others down here.

He did believe that God loved him and cared about him. How much, he didn't know.

What a way to think about others! Everyone, white, black, brown, easy, hard, or in-between is my brother or sister? Chip mused.

Even if he was not all-in with church, he was willing to accept that God loved him, knew him, and knew others too, everyone else on the planet. And if we are all part of God's family, Chip reasoned, then he could try thinking of others in his life as his extended family.

Maybe helping others, like he did all those years ago, without thinking about what he would get out of the situation, would make him and maybe others a little bit bigger, stronger, kinder.

Chip knew he needed a little bit of all of that in his life, and so he was willing to give it a go.

He would change. He didn't know if he could do this, but he would try. There was something missing in his life and he knew he wanted more of what he experienced when he was younger, innocent, less calloused.

He wanted to feel that love again, and he would feel that love again by being kind to others, his brothers, and sisters.

He would be more outward-focused than inward-focused – a better, stronger Chip!

Chapter 19

New Trajectories

John died three days later.

It came as a shock to everyone except Claire. She had known for quite a while that he could go any day but had kept it to herself and their immediate family which numbered five grown children, their spouses, and no less than 16 grandchildren, the oldest being a rebellious 19-year-old who would only listen to his granddad and no one else.

John passed without pain in his home with family around him. He was able to spend time with each of his family members, including his grandchildren, saying his last words to them, things he wanted them to remember after he was gone.

John was at peace with himself when he died; he and Claire had come to terms with his terminal illness.

After his first round of chemo was complete and he was into his second, it was obvious his days and weeks were numbered. So, John did what he always did – he carried on with his friends and associates, like Chip, as if everything were okay.

John's funeral service was held on a Sunday morning on the first weekend in May. The weather was unseasonably cold and crisp, but the sun shined brightly.

Hundreds turned out for the service, most of whom wanted to tell Claire and her family how John had touched them, inspired them with their own personal stories.

They shared how John had said things to them in their darkest hours, their moments of loneliness and despair that had been the turning points in their lives.

Many of them spoke of John in terms reserved for saints or angels, someone that had given them hope, encouragement, light, and pulled them out from the shadows.

When Chip got the news, he felt an immediate dull pain take up lodging in his heart. The pain was, he was sure of it, a recognition that part of him had left, gone somewhere else.

Chip wasn't sure there was a heaven, but if there was, John was there, waiting for others to join him.

Chip cried like a child and knew where he should be on Sunday morning – honoring a man who had made such an impact on his life or, at least, was about to.

At the service, one young woman quoted Pope Francis in describing what John had meant to her and her husband when they were going through their own struggles and John had reached out to them. She read slowly and through her tears,

> *Rivers do not drink their own fruit; the sun does not shine on itself, and flowers do not spread their fragrance for themselves. Living for others is a rule of nature. We are all born to help each other. No matter how difficult it is…Life is good when you are happy but much better when others are happy because of you.*

Monday

Chip came to work early that morning. His goal was simple for that day – focus on others and what they need, not what you need.

He would be kind to everyone and through in a few, anonymous, kind acts. He was going to be a better version of himself today. Chip was going to honor John today, and honoring John meant helping others. He didn't have to wait long.

Yvonka was another accountant, like Chip, on the fourth-floor. Chip tried to avoid her most of the time until he couldn't because he thought she was a little too intense for him on most days of the week. Make that all days of the week if he could work it right.

Yvonka was the loud one in the group. She had something to prove, maybe everything to prove, and Chip preferred to keep his head down when voices were raised during group meetings when Yvonka was in the mix.

Chip didn't do confrontational very well, but Yvonka did. She did it like she was paid to do it. To her, everything was a battle where there was a singular winner (her) and losers (everyone else). And it didn't matter what was up for discussion: the news of the day, who was in line first for the coffee, which seat to take during the weekly conference calls, etc.

The seating location of the conference calls particularly irritated Chip because it was a conference call with speakers conveniently placed along the table and along the room walls. So no matter where you sat, people could hear you. Yvonka always sat on Peter's right, as if she was the enforcer for all of management's edicts.

Yvonka grated on Chip and Yvonka didn't know it because she had long assessed Chip as a non-threat in her threat matrix of those that could compete with her for a management job. Chip was under the radar and barely noticed by Yvonka until now.

They met, almost bumped into each other, in the hallway approaching the main door into their work area. The glass door was heavy and was not one of those automatic ones that opened when you came within x feet of it. No, this one had to be opened manually and not without some effort.

Chip and Yvonka came out of the elevator together but not speaking. Yvonka didn't speak unless she had a point to make, an ax to grind, or someone to push under a metaphorical bus.

Chip quickened his pace to the door; he had to get there first. Yvonka, noticing everything, picked up her pace. They were both progressed to a speed walk of sorts, but their facial expressions remained neutral.

Chip made it to the door first, slightly out of breath but elated. He pushed through the door and held it open for Yvonka who had the rare gift of being able to walk without looking down, fixated on her object, in this case Chip. She stopped at the opened door and spoke in measured tone to Chip, "You don't have to open the door for me, Chip. Go ahead." Her body was erect and her feet were fixed on the door's threshold.

Chip's arms were quivering, slightly but visibly. The door was heavy and his adrenaline had been activated.

"Oh no, I insist, Yvonka. Go ahead, happy Monday!" Chip was smiling; he was thinking about John and about how Yvonka is one of his sisters, how everyone he would meet today would be one of his brothers or sisters.

He was thinking about John when he burst out of that elevator, walked the hallway, and was holding that door open for another.

"I don't need someone to open the door for me," she said, and Chip heard the familiar bite in her voice.

Yvonka wasn't moving and a line was forming behind her from others that had arrived to find themselves at an impasse in the form of a smiling Chip and a stoic, confident Yvonka. Chip had an audience. What he said next came out quickly and rushed but with heart.

"Hear me out, Yvonka. My friend, John, died the other day. I think we all know him," Chip said, ensuring his voice carried to the small crowd of ten, puzzled co-workers behind Yvonka, lined up in a single file like they were boarding an airplane.

Yvonka hadn't blinked yet.

"Well, he taught me something. He said if I focused less on myself and more on others, I could have a small part in helping someone have a better day. I just wanted to do something nice this morning."

Chip took a breath.

The crowd was mesmerized; they hadn't heard Chip talk like that before. Yvonka was thinking – Chip could tell by how her mouth moved, but her lips remained closed. Then she spoke, but without the edge or the bite, "My grandma used to tell me that all the time." Yvonka smiled at Chip, a warm smile. There was no contest anymore, only understanding and a little warmth between them.

"You know, you're right, Chip," Yvonka said and then turned to the single file of Monday-morning co-workers behind her. "Chip's right. My grandma was right. Thanks, Chip," she said and walked through the door with less purpose but more natural movement.

Yvonka had a different morning and a different afternoon following the Chip Clementine episode. She was patient with others, did not interrupt them when they said something in two sentences that they could have said in one.

She didn't fuss where she sat in a meeting, and she didn't crack any jokes at someone else's expense. She even complimented a colleague who had stumbled through a presentation he gave to Yvonka and the rest of her team. Yvonka hadn't complimented anyone at work ever.

Each night, she wrote everything of importance in her journal and would write that the 'Clementine Door' morning event (that's how she labeled it) brought back memories from her childhood.

She remembered her grandma, someone she hadn't thought about in a long time.

She thought about her kind words and how she wanted to be like her when she grew up. She wrote how she felt that rest of the day.

It would be this day, years later, when she was running her own company, that she would tell others that was the day when she turned a corner in her life and had become a better listener, a forgiving daughter, a more-accepting leader, a better human being.

And, for this moment, she had a non-descript, middle-aged accountant called Chip Clementine to thank.

Later that Evening

Chip arrived at his brother's house with an armful of avocados and nothing else. Rick opened the door only after the passcode was whispered through the door – his rules. Chip walked through and was quick to the point.

"Rick, you were right. Avocados are the answer," Chip said in a slower, quieter conversational tone than usual.

At Rick's house, Chip was careful to not make any sudden movements and certainly no physical contact. Rick who was easily startled and some of their prior visits had been measured in seconds.

Rick was partially right about avocados. Rick's advice to Chip when Chip first told him about Chip's cancer diagnosis last fall had, at first, been received with skepticism.

In the months since the diagnosis, Chip kept his diet very routine, non-adventurous. His only addition was avocados, upon the advice of his older brother.

By now, Chip was avocadoed out but knew he had to try something new with his brother, find a way to connect with him better, especially after he came back from his last tour in Iraq.

Who would have thought what one can do with avocados? Of course, there was the guacamole dip, the avocado on toast, and even avocado-infused mineral water – those were the safe options.

But safe options only last so long, and three weeks into his avocado regime back in October, he had ventured out, maybe a bit too far, but ventured nonetheless.

He tried his hand at avocado ice-cream which was an epic fail and then went to what he thought might work – jam combinations. Mixing avocado with fruit was a gamble. And, true to form, attempting to create a breakfast jam with avocado sent him and any others that would try it with him down culinary rabbit trails with equally disastrous results.

There was avocado and strawberry, avocado and grape, and, finally, avocado and avocado, which was a highly concentrated version of regular avocado, which still didn't work on toast or anything else.

Through trial and error, Chip arrived at the same conclusion he had started out with – avocado on toast with a little pepper and a dash of salt.

Of course, it took a couple of weeks for him to get there, but when he settled on how avocados could work for him moving forward, he never looked back.

And, now, he was here to thank Rick and try something else with him. They were both still by the door, but Chip had made it inside barely.

Rick was staring at his brother. Chip would have to make the next move; this was probably a low-energy day for Rick, and on low-energy days, he did only two things – play videogames with his online gamer buddies and drink caffeine-spiked, energy drinks, preferably green ones.

"Hey, isn't this game day?" Chip inquired, acting surprised, like he had just remembered something.

"Yeah, why?" Rick was also surprised but for a different reason. Chip never played games with him, ever. Not even board games.

Rick had never seen Chip take even a remote interest in anything electronic, holographic, virtual. Chip liked to read non-fiction and how-to manuals – that was it.

"I want to give this thing a go, you know, fight the undead and all that," Chip said, picking up Rick's guest virtual reality/gaming headset.

Chip picked it up the wrong way; Rick noticed but didn't grimace the way he did when his girlfriend picked it up like that the last time someone wanted to enter his gaming world.

"Tonight, there's no undead, just a pack of velociraptors in a jungle we have to find and kill. It's a search-and-destroy mission.

"We get in, we get out. They broke through their security perimeter and have been seen moving toward the other side of the island where the tourists are.

"We helicopter in as a team, track them down, neutralize them, and collect the money from the game park owners. That's the mission. You in?"

Rick was matter-of-fact. Underneath, he was really liking the idea that his brother would be with him.

"When you say neutralize, you mean catch them, right?" Chip asked, just for clarification.

"No, I mean kill them. We will have M-4 assault rifles with laser scopes and modified, high-caliber rounds. There's no catching." Rick did not have much time to go over the basics before the team would assemble online. He needed a commitment. "You in or not?"

"Yeah, I'm in," Chip said excitedly.

Two hours in and Chip knew the basics of working and fighting and surviving in a virtual-reality world. It was a world of cunning, vicious raptors on the hunt for tourists and Rick's team had to stop them before it was too late.

Chip learned how to walk, crawl, run, jump, look left, look right, crouch, duck, and shoot his assault rifle (and reload it).

There were a lot of firsts that evening. Firing a rifle in a virtual world was liberating. Chip had never fired a gun before and did imaginary recoil actions with his shoulder each time he fired just because he could and felt like that was probably what would happen if he was firing a real weapon.

Chip had never experienced anything like this before. Putting on that headset, he never would have imagined how utterly immersive his new environment was.

He didn't think he was in Rick's living room anymore; the sounds, the vibrations, it all felt so real.

The team of six of them had assembled on the helicopter pad near the park's luxury marina, and Chip watched as Rick greeted his teammates and the way they talked to each other.

They were part of his family. It was clear that several of them were from his old army unit where they had all served together.

Of course, Chip was the new guy, and new guys run point on all patrols, they said to him as they loaded onto the H-60 Blackhawk helicopter loaded down with their weapons, ammunition, and rucksacks.

Chip thought they (we) all looked an impressive sight as the helicopter started to rise above the marina and moved out over the high, electrical fence into the triple canopy jungle and the velociraptors that were, no doubt, waiting for them.

The first few minutes into the game were uneventful. They were dropped off in the middle of the park in a long valley with high grass.

They walked their pre-programmed routes, with Chip in front, who was happy to be there but totally clueless about what to do if they were attacked.

Then they heard the click-click noise and everyone took a knee and set up a hasty security perimeter.

Rick's little tutorial in his living room with Chip didn't mention what a perimeter was, let alone a hasty one, so Chip kept walking out in front like he had done since they had watched the helicopter fly off and leave them alone.

Then Chip saw three of them out in the distance, about 100 meters, coming right at them. Rick was the first one to Chip and told Chip to crouch down and watch for a possible side attack from other raptors in the pack while Rick took out the three approaching ones.

The noise was deafening; Rick was an amazing shot, and Chip saw all three raptors tumble to the ground as each was shot through the upper torso or head with single, rapid fire from Rick's rifle which was anything but virtual in Chip's mind.

Chip turned back to his 'sector' just in time to see one raptor approaching him and Rick at breakneck speed.

Chip pointed his weapon in the general direction and pulled the trigger. Chip's weapon was on fully automatic and thirty rounds hit the raptor center mass. Accountant turned mercenary, Chip had dropped a raptor just twenty feet from where they were standing.

Chip's hands were shaking in real life, so his virtual hands replicated those actions for all to see. In real life, he was sweating and he may have lost control of his bladder for a moment, but the virtual gaming monitors had not picked up on those particulars and, for that, he was grateful.

"Nice job, Chip," one of the others said. "You totally saved Rick from getting side swiped."

Rick was visibly impressed with Chip.

Rick gave him a virtual hug and the others high-fived him. The mission didn't need to go till eleven. They had met their objectives, collected their virtual cash and gaming points, and figured out what their next mission would be the following week.

Chip was invited. He declined. Chip needed a few weeks to make sense of it all but would probably come back in later in the month.

They understood, especially for a first-timer. When they said their goodbyes and each signed off, Rick and Chip could see their virtual teammates slowly evaporate from their virtual world. Then, they looked at each other and the headsets came off. They were back in the living room they had never left.

Rick stared at Chip with pride. Chip didn't know if he could sum up what he had been through – there were too many adjectives and not enough nouns. But he did know what this meant for him and Rick.

"I want to do that again, Rick, but only if we are on the same team. Is this what it felt like when you were in the army with your buddies out there in Iraq?" Chip wanted to know. *Maybe Rick would tell him something, open up, anything would be something*, Chip thought.

Rick took a long time to answer, but when he did, Chip knew they were both in a better place with each other.

"I just feel like I'm doing something real, something important when I am with the team, you know, like I can contribute, do something positive. I know it's just dinosaurs or zombies, but they are the side show. I just like being with my friends together in something like this."

Then, after a long pause, he spoke again. "If you want to get me, really get, this is how, Chip. I'm not that complicated," Rick said.

Until that evening, Chip had not fired a gun or been attacked by anything that wanted to hurt him. His time with Rick and the rest of the team on a remote, steamy island with raptors had been more about bonding and understanding Rick.

"Rick," said Chip. "My Tuesday nights are free usually, and I would love to join the team if you'll have me," he said hopefully. Rick's response was unexpected since it came with a big hug and emotion.

"Man! Definitely! This will be great. I can teach you so much more about tactics and stuff," said Rick. He was so happy, so thrilled. His eyes were alive.

Chip knew this was a new beginning for both of them, and with a little more training with grappling hooks and high explosives, he knew he could do more for Rick and the team than be the token-point guy/human bait on future missions.

Chip had found a way to reach Rick and make a connection, and that was more than enough for now.

Thursday Night

Thursday night at the Clementine's house was 'Spaghetti Night' which sounded more fun than it actually was. The sauce was out of the can and the meat cooked without love.

The garlic bread was readymade and microwaved; the salad was lettuce and tomatoes. The salad dressing was Italian, always Italian.

Keeping the menu the same made the grocery shopping simple. Simple was quick, and when it came to eating, quick was preferred.

They had given up being creative with their cuisine early in their marriage when they both realized neither one of them were talented in the kitchen. But they didn't have a lot of disposable income either.

Most nights of the week were at home, and Fridays were reserved for dining out and always at the same Mexican restaurant where Chip would order his carnitas fajitas and she would order her chicken chimichanga.

Each Friday night at the Mexican restaurant was less about the food and more about a celebration of the end of another dull and uneventful week together.

Marriage for them was comfortable and routine which translated to predictable and safe.

So many things between them were left unsaid, enough to keep them bottled up and pushed down and glossed over each day and each night.

Chip knew this and so did she. But life marched on and the days turned into weeks, the weeks and months into years, and, before they knew it, they accepted what they had as their new normal.

In the years since their kids had grown up and left to marry and live their own lives, Chip and his wife had become comfortable, too comfortable with what they had between themselves.

The spaghetti tasted exactly the same as last Tuesday. They had eaten slowly and were finishing up their Tuesday night dessert – apple cobbler without the cinnamon. Chip asked a singular, simple question that would change their marriage.

"Want to go out for a walk?" Chip asked with a smile and a face full of hope.

"A what?" she asked, surprised. She wasn't used to questions; their conversations were usually just statements and responses, usually responses.

"Let's go out for a walk right now. The weather's nice and I think it would be good for us to walk after our dinners. What d'ya say?" Chip asked.

Say something about the humidity...Chip liked humidity...humidity lubricated the joints...

"Urr, sure," she said awkwardly. They had never gone out for a walk after dinner. They had walked together before, but it was to get from point A to point B. Walking after dinner seemed to her there would be no destination, no stopping point, just walking.

They put on their light jackets, locked the front door, and left for a walk around the neighborhood, their neighborhood where they had bought their first house together.

As they turned the corner of the first block, Chip held his wife's hand gently. His hands were warm. She thought, *this is nice. Different but nice.*

The conversation started off easier than he thought it would. They talked about their children, how fast they had grown, who they married, where they lived, how they were different from each other, the struggles they had, how much they loved them, and how much they missed them.

All of their children had grown up, married, and moved out of state because that was where the jobs were. They did come to visit occasionally, but how they wished the occasionally would turn to frequently.

When the last of the kids graduated from high school and went off to college, they felt like they lost their purpose, their *raison d'être*.

As they walked, the motion made it easier to speak, to share. There was no agenda on this walk; both wanted to see how far they would go and how long they would be out.

There was no competition, only curiosity between themselves. They admired the trees, the greenway, the neighborhood park – how green, how vibrant, how real, how rejuvenating.

They felt healthier, more connected as they walked, not a brisk pace but a leisurely one. As they walked more, they started to talk about their feelings toward each other. Chip told his wife he loved her and she made him stop when he said it.

"It's been so long since you said that," she said. It wasn't an accusation, a criticism. Chip didn't take it any other way.

He knew he didn't say it often enough, didn't show it either. But he also knew that she was his rock, his kindred spirit, and that they had walked this journey together for so long and he needed her to know how much he cared about her.

She told him she loved him, and they embraced on the corner of Elm Street in a neighborhood that looked like most other street corners in a town not too different from most. Talking was easier between them out on that walk.

The subjects were still hard, but they were more at ease bringing them up in the first place, and that was a first in the Clementine house.

When they returned to their home, things were different now. Each wanted to do more things together with the other; no more retreating and no more hiding.

They took more risks because they trusted more. And because they trusted more, over the days and weeks that followed, there were changes in the Clementine house.

New dinner menus were created. Mexican food was put on hold for a while and replaced with Asian fusion. Chip's pet tortoise, Horace, was given full family member status and rights.

This meant Horace was granted full access to any room in the house, even if it took him a couple of weeks to get to a room of his choosing.

They went out on date nights, mostly cooking classes and walks around parks.

They set up calls with their kids and their families and found some money in their budget to schedule their vacations with them, instead of opting for their go-to cruise line for a cruise with others like them, miserable, alone, and disengaged.

The following week.

Chip knew this was a work in progress and that there were parts of him that would not change so quickly and that was okay.

At his core, Chip continued to control more and more of his life and guard against randomness despite his on-going efforts to think of others' interests

203

and needs before his own, to think of others as his brothers or sisters, and to be kinder, more thoughtful.

Earlier in May, Chip was promoted to assistant project manager, a permanent promotion as opposed to the earlier one he received which was temporary and probationary and which had lasted a day or two at the most.

Chip didn't question why or how he earned the promotion, but he took it in style and with only one condition.

He wanted to decorate his new office his way. And his way meant an office with no walls or doors, just a chair and a desk in the middle of a work area surrounded by other managers with normal offices.

He needed the folks who reported to him to know that he was accessible. Accessibility was the new currency of leadership, thought Chip. But if accessibility was currency, it was spent quickly, for a price was paid for Chip's brilliant idea, namely loss of privacy.

Chip found out pretty quickly how easily others could hear his conversations that were supposed to be privileged and confidential. But since Chip had no walls and no doors, everyone could hear what he said to his leadership such as bonus recommendations or personnel issues of a highly delicate nature.

Chip was easily distracted by his former colleagues that would walk by his 'space' formerly known as an office and casually mention things, knowing that Chip would hear them.

He was more distracted than most because his rise up the corporate ladder had resulted in a corresponding decrease in workload since other people now did the heavy lifting. So, Chip had more time on his hands to think and ponder how to be kinder to others.

Still, his rise in corporate America hadn't been as fast as others, but he had paid his dues and, at times, had gone to great lengths to convince others he was hardworking, smart, engaged.

Chip, if he was honest with himself, was barely working, moderately intelligent, and adrift most of the time. He was able to fool most with a few, well-tried tricks of the trade. It wasn't that Chip was lazy, it's just that he knew his limits.

He knew that anything asked of him past three p.m. was wishful thinking. So, years ago, he'd taken one of his work jackets and permanently placed it on the back of his chair, so, when he quietly left early, others would think he was still working.

He always got a chuckle in the breakroom when he overhead others whispering that Chip Clementine never goes home and has no life. If only they knew.

Chip would spend the last fifteen minutes of his day creating a false narrative. He would disorganize his desk and everything on it to convey he was in the middle of something.

The lights were never turned off. And, of course, a sign on the door, read 'In meeting – back at _____ (he let them fill it in).'

Chip would write in the time with different color markers and the time would always be different but never before 4:30 p.m. and never after 5:30 p.m.

Another thing he mastered was to accept all meeting invites, whether they conflicted with other meetings.

He frequently triple-booked his calendar but always attended each meeting for at least ten minutes before saying he had to leave because he was, well, triple booked.

Triple-booked sounded so much better than double-booked. And he would be called out if he said quadruple-booked, so he kept it within reason.

To be seen as someone who valued being pushed to the limits through demanding exercise, Chip placed a soaking wet T-shirt on a hangar in his office, right after lunch, in prominent view.

Others would think he had skipped lunch to run a brisk six-miler instead of eating. He wanted others to think he had priorities when he didn't – not even close.

Chip rolled his sleeves and loosened his tie in the afternoon. He had come through chemo, willing to try new things and maybe throw out others.

He started to think about how much vacation time he had and if he could convince Laura (Mrs. Clementine) to take a few months and go with him out west to Alaska for some commercial fishing outings.

He would call them outings to soften the blow, but he was getting itchy to feel salt on his skin. Maybe it was time for something else?

Chip leaned back and fell sideways, catching one of the leg chairs on his rug. Everyone saw him fall, since he had no office, just open space, and rushed to his aid.

He was okay, but when he got up, there was a conviction and purpose in Chip on what he would do next.

The End

CPSIA information can be obtained
at www.ICGtesting.com
Printed in the USA
BVHW041333251021
619819BV00002B/13